A Witch's Sorrow

A Witch's Sorrow

Callie Rae Sutton

First paperback edition Oct 2023

Cover design by Amy Hunter
Edited by Mary E. Porter
Formatted by Kari Holloway

ISBN Paperback 979-8-9885539-2-2
ISBN Ebook 979-8-9885539-3-9

www.blushingcrow13.com

Forward

Death. The word seems hollow in meaning—void of attachment, simply part of life. The word "loss", however, has heartstrings attached. I tie an emotion to this feeling. When we lose someone, we often ask a multitude of questions: Why now? Why so young? Why them? Unfortunately, we never seem to get answers to these questions, and yet they haunt us as we grieve.

This year, I lost someone very dear to me. Though I have lost family in the past, this was different. Losing someone when you are an adult raises more questions, imposes more anger, and includes a different outlook on life than when you lose someone as a child. I lost both my Papa and Grandma when I was a teenager. My small world crumbled and even to this day, I miss them both terribly. Their outlook on life was kind to no end…accepting, while keeping true to their beliefs and values, unlike so many of us.

My aunt was the same——a firm believer in her faith and never turned down an opportunity to help anyone in any way. She passed far too soon. I wrote this passage in her honor:

"The light of the world has significantly dimmed due to the loss of such a brilliant soul as Aunt Lesley. She had genuine warmth and kindness in her heart and shared it with everyone. From her family to her church, her friends, to her (Church group of) girls. Her love truly overflowed in abundance.

Unfortunately, it has been my experience that those are the ones who leave us first. You'd think it would be the other way around, and when it's not, you're left wondering if the key to a long life is to be spiteful, unforgiving, and selfish. It's when I feel this anger that I can hear my aunt's voice telling me she wouldn't have had it any other way. That to live a long life of hateful darkness isn't much of a life at all, but to share such a light, even if it is far too short, is one worth living.

We never know the extent of the impact of a life until it disappears. And yet, I know for a fact that Aunt Lesley touched so many of our lives.

My wish to you all is to live your life with a simple fraction of the love my aunt had for you so her spirit can live on and together we might help make up for just a portion of her resounding loss."

Death seems to hold different meanings in a variety of cultures. In general, Christianity, for example, preaches that at the end of time, there will be a day of judgment at which time we are all judged by God. In addition, overall, death is seen as the end of one's life here on Earth. People are then judged by God, and Jesus, God's son, intercedes so that believers' souls shall live in peace in Heaven or in strife in Hell for non-believers.

Ancient Egyptians, among others, believed if you did enough good to outbalance the bad in your life, you would continue living in the afterlife. They were often buried with their worldly possessions so that they could continue living with those same riches.

Some believe we are living in Hell now, or that after we die, that's it. Our body is returned to the earth, and our soul dies with our bodies.

Another concept of death is reincarnation, which I find to be a soothing concept. The opportunity to not only right our wrongs in another life, but to once again live with those whom we love is comforting to me. The thought of our birthmarks indicating how we have died in the past, or meeting someone so young with an "old soul" piques my interest, and inevitably, drags me into a spiral of questions and outcomes.

I wrote this book with simply one reincarnation concept: a view in which reincarnation is a curse of sorts—never fully at peace as it cycles life after life. This was the only full manuscript my aunt read before she passed even though she had read my previous published poems and some of my short stories. Although I know her faith never landed near reincarnation itself, she had faith in me, and offered insight and acceptance in the story itself. And for that, I am forever grateful.

I miss you, Aunt Lesley. I will love you forever...until we meet again.

Preface

Selena stood in front of a broken piece of mirror to prepare herself for her speech to her subjects. But as she closed her eyes, she cringed with every hollow echo of dripping water streaming from the ceiling's cracks in her chambers. As she took in a deep breath, her nose flared at the potent staleness that always hung in the air—never was there a breeze of reprieve. Forcing the air out of her lungs, she heard a knock at the door. When it opened, the collective whispers of her people begged for a hope that had been long overdue. And finally, she had the last piece to carry out her plan.

Selena's escort, the one who had knocked, bowed his head, then reported, "Everyone has gathered, my queen. We are ready for you."

Nodding her head, Selena waited for the door to close, then she turned to the opposing door that was tucked into a tight nook and closed off to her underground palace. The scratching from the other side gave Selena the confidence boost she needed to greet her people, and she smiled with the knowledge of what was about to begin. "The last piece is here. Our time has come."

Selena walked out of her chambers. The mumbling amongst the crowd below died to a murmur as a wave of bows rippled before her. She waited until all were upright before she spoke. "It has been years—too many to count—since the wizard cast us fairies underground. And for what? I'd hardly think this qualifies as survival."

The crowd roared.

"When we needed food, we begged and settled for the crumbs that fell from the humans' tables. When we needed shelter, we took some twigs from their firewood storage." Selena's anger at the initial cruelty toward her kind and their current living conditions made her stomach boil and churn with rage.

Water droplets pierced through the tiny holes in the soil above. The air flow was stifling, creating a humidity which drained every ounce of energy they had left. As a result, it contributed to an abundance of unnecessary illnesses.

Selena gazed upon her subjects' weathered faces. "It's time for us to take back what is rightfully ours. I have created a darkness that will wipe out the human race for good. Soon, we will bring that darkness into the light!" Cheers burst through the crowd.

Selena waved at the cheering fairies below, then turned and headed back to her chambers.

A bloomed yellow daffodil cup sat in the center of her room. As she walked to it, she remembered the good old days when flying would have been her mode of transportation. Ever since the banishment underground, their source of fairy dust, the sun's rays, was no longer available to them, so they had no other choice but to move via the mundane mode of walking.

Selena bustled about, knocking bottles off their shelves. She grabbed a couple of dead roses and slashed off the thorns and poured them into the delicate daffodil cup. After purposefully slicing her hand, she squeezed her thick, black blood into the flower and used the thornless rose stem like a wooden spoon to stir.

Once her hand stopped spilling blood, she went to the back of her room and opened the little door where the scratching sounds had been constant. A rat that Selena had deprived of water scurried out and immediately began drinking from the flower's bowl. After all the poisoned liquid was gone, minus the one drop which acted as an anchor in the center of the flower, the rat keeled over.

"Splendid!" Selena rubbed her hands together, almost simulating a rat when cleansing itself. "But now isn't the time to slumber, dear pet. We have work to do."

Selena removed the lid of one jar she had procured earlier. "Pixie Dust". Since no fairy, including the queen, was able to generate any dust since the banishment, Selena had saved some dust and sequestered it into a jar for a rainy day such as this. She poured the gold dust into her hand. Her heart fluttered at the weightlessness of it. Her blood jolted with a rush of adrenaline just by looking at it.

Selena bent down next to the lifeless rodent and blew the dust onto its corpse, then whispered into its ear. The rat sprung back to life, and without hesitation ran out of the hole from whence it came.

The rat shared its sickness with all the others of its kind. They all scattered amongst the humans, biting anyone in their path. All Selena had to do now was to wait—wait for the Black Death to wipe out the mortals.

Almost a year had gone by since Selena released the sickness and she and her court were able to resurface. She wanted to witness the suffering of the pathetic human beings, study the process of her plague, and examine the damage it had on the victims.

Selena stood at the edge of a town next to her forest, their new home until the humans were gone. She remembered when she had first broken ground, returning to the top where she belonged. The crisp, unoppressive air stung with her first breath, like being stabbed with an icicle. But the recovery was quick, cooling her blood and running its course like a dancing stream in winter.

The streets weren't vacant, yet death loomed around every corner. Some houses were empty, with nothing but a rank odor that seeped out of the stony, cracked foundation. Families abandoned family members, leaving bodies of the dead as people feared they, too, would catch the illness if they got too close. Ash piles of burnt corpses lay in dark alleyways from those who were brave enough to gather the decaying bodies.

Selena was rather pleased with herself as she witnessed the decay and destruction she had caused.

As the months drudged on, she allowed more and more of her subjects to resurface—granting "outings" into town from the forest—so that they could also marvel at their queen's success.

"Keep a low profile for now. Your dust will replenish, but restrain from using any for the time being. Observe and report back to me, then recoil into the forest." The fairies, still in their human form, overjoyed for their moment of freedom, surveyed the town to please their queen.

"The humans are fleeing to the countryside, hoping to leave this darkness behind them," a faithful servant reported.

"Let them. It'll catch up to them, eventually. We must be patient. It'll all be ours."

"Yes, my queen." The servant bowed as she walked backwards, leaving Selena's company.

Selena visited the edge of the dying village to see the humans' pathetic escape attempt for herself. There wasn't a road that wasn't packed with a lot of terrified, desperate people.

On one particular road stood a man who seemed to be examining the townspeople.

What is this? Selena could tell this man, though human, was not without power. *Perhaps a witch has finally stumbled in my path.* His eyes were soft when he spoke to these people. Selena sauntered over to the intriguing man.

"Hello," she greeted.

He failed to respond.

"What are you doing?"

"I'm ensuring the townspeople are free of infection. If I see no signs, then they can retreat into the country, escape this evil, and live out their lives as fully as they can, given the tragedy they have seen here."

"Why?"

"Why what?" The man's eyebrows furrowed, and he cocked his head while still examining someone.

"Why are you helping them?" Selena snapped.

The man stood and looked at Selena for the first time.

Captivating, he thought as the woman drew him in with her beauty.

"Well?" Selena persisted.

He blinked and jolted out of his star-struck trance, then answered, "Why wouldn't I? I do my best to help them. These people are innocent, and this sickness is destroying families."

"I don't know if 'innocent' is the right word. And you have power. Why waste your time on these simple beings?"

He dragged her away from his patients. "You go first."

The man's body quaked. *How did she know I have power? What does that make her?* The questions flooded his mind.

"Oh, relax." Selena brushed his hand away, signaling him to release his grip on her. "My name is Selena. I have power as well."

"I'm Lucian. Technically a warlock, but I prefer the term healer. I don't really follow suit with the darkness of others of my kind. I use energy from the surrounding nature and help those who are in need." He glanced back over to the people who waited for him; they shivered in the permanently damp atmosphere.

"Again, I ask why? You don't know these people." Selena placed her hands on his chest, closed her eyes, and felt the warmth emanating from his heart. She leaned into him. Her breath bounced off his neck when she whispered into his ear, "You are powerful, I can tell. You aren't weak like they are."

Lucian smacked his hands upward between Selena's hands, forcing her to take a step back. "I have a soul as well. I'm not going to just stand by and watch innocent people die."

"You are intriguing." Selena bit her bottom lip, eyeing him from head to toe.

Lucian stared back at her. He watched as she questioned his kindness towards these people. *Was she really that heartless?* "Come here, let me show you something."

They walked over to a child, the little girl next in line. Selena noticed a woman on the opposing side of where they stood. The woman had her hands pressed into a prayer. She placed her fingertips against her lips. Water pooled in the woman's eyes, ready to drop at any moment. Selena returned her attention to Lucian and the child. He looked over the child's body carefully.

"What are you looking for?" Selena asked him, wondering what her plague did to the bodies.

"Blackness, boils, bumps of any kind. I feel their skin to see if they are too warm, and check their throats for lumps. I can tell if it is this deadly sickness or if it is simply a temporary illness that will fade on its own. If it is anything but the Black Death, then I heal them so that they don't get killed by their families later under false pretenses."

"How can you tell the difference?"

"The plague has an evil I can feel——a slow burning pulse of broken glass crashing into me in waves."

Selena faintly smiled, ensuring no one could see how proud she was of her work.

Lucian finished examining the child. He nodded to her, giving her permission to cross the invisible line of life or death. The girl flew to her mother. The relief from the mother was palpable, forcing the welled tears the mother had been holding to fall down her cheeks. She lifted her child off the ground and spun her in a circle. The scene overwhelmed Selena. She had just witnessed pure love and joy, and her heart twinged in a way it never had before.

Selena grabbed a handful of her dust and flung it up into the air. It ballooned into a radiant, golden light, and the world around her stopped. She studied the mother and child who clung to each other as if not even the moon's gravity could separate them. A tear managed to escape the mother's eye before the world froze and Selena took notice.

"I thought crying was solely from pain…"

"It is sometimes."

Selena looked around. "Lucian, you didn't freeze."

"No. I protected myself when people started getting sick. Tears of joy are very real, and there isn't another love like that of a mother and her child."

A lifetime of bitterness had made Selena who she was; nonetheless, Selena felt her heart soften. She felt some strange kind of feeling…a likeness for the concept of a family. "Thank you for sharing this…for showing…love."

The world slowly shifted as her magic faded, and yet Selena and Lucian stood as still as statues. This man had given Selena something no other being had offered.

Transfixed, Lucian could see a future life with this woman, making a family of his own.

"Will you marry me?" Selena blurted. She only halfway knew what she said. She didn't fully have control of her heart at that moment.

"Yes," Lucian responded with no breath lingering between their words.

"Good. I'll be right back," Selena assured as she ran towards the country woods, which she knew all too well. Going back into the earth didn't seem as bad as it once had. Back in her old chambers lay the daffodil that had started it all. A single drop of death remained, the anchor to the sickness. Selena picked up the stem she had used to stir the concoction and placed its base in the droplet. The thirsty stem drank it and sprouted thorns. Multiple rosebuds blossomed from the now black stem as it soaked up the darkness. Selena threw her dust onto the stem and watched as it intertwined into a crown.

She placed the crown on top of her head, making it invisible to all but her fellow fairies. Selena had found love, and nothing, not even her own wickedness, was going to spoil that gift.

She ran back out to join Lucian, who found no more signs of the sickness that day. And within a few weeks, the plague had disappeared from this region of the world, and soon enough, it would be eradicated entirely. Peace was being restored, and how better to celebrate than to have a wedding?

It was a mystical adventure, one neither would ever forget. Little did Lucian know that the evening's events would change his life forever.

After the ceremony, the couple visited the local inn and asked for a room.

"I'm going to put on something more comfortable." Selena's wedding updo unraveled, allowing her long black hair to fall to the ground. Her translucent purple-tinged wings stretched out; the golden tips sparkled in the moonlight that shone through the window. The wedding dress turned black, accented with a purple belt and a golden crown that was decorated in tiny, red rosebuds and thorns that looked like the Black Death itself, yet beautiful nonetheless.

"What are you?" Lucian said as he backed away from his new wife.

"The Queen of the Dark Fairies. Sorry for not telling you, but I wanted a family, like the one you showed me." Selena inched forward to Lucian, arms outstretched.

Lucian kept backing up until he hit the wall. "That's a prohibited venture. Magic laws about interspecies procreation are irrevocably clear."

"Lucian, I know we are married now, but unfortunately for you, I'm not asking for permission. You mortals have to get messy while creating a family. I, however, do not. I just need a teensy bit of your blood, love. Then I can drink up, and boom…family in moments."

"It's still not right."

"Yes, well, I am the Queen of the Dark Fairies, so excuse me for not always following the rules."

Selena pinched off a bud from her thorny crown, crushed it into a powder, and sprinkled it into her goblet that she had just made visible in her hand. She offered her hand to Lucian, as a sign he was now needed. Lucian stared at her with his dark green eyes. He realized there was no way of him winning a fight with his new wife. *What did I get myself into?* He ran his fingers through his wavy, ink black hair then reluctantly strode over to Selena.

"That's a good husband. Now hold still while I retrieve your sample," she patronized as she cut his hand with a blade and squeezed the beautiful red, rich blood into her goblet. Lucian pulled away, but Selena held his hand firm. "More…just in case." After a few more seconds, she let him go, then brushed her fingertips together, letting her golden glitter heal Lucian's hand. "I know it's in my nature to be evil, but I do love you, Lucian. We vowed to take care of each other, and I intend to uphold my end."

"Of course." He wasn't expecting her kindness, but was still concerned about being caught. "How will we hide?"

"There's an old tree deep in the woods. It used to be my home when I was a young pixie. You can protect the tree with a spell from wandering eyes and protect our family. You warlocks are good at protection spells."

"That can work. When do we leave?"

Selena walked back over to Lucian and held his hand. She gazed into his piercing eyes. She loved how they pulled her in…entranced her. No one had captivated her like he did. The thought of finding true love had never crossed her mind in her whole long life…until now.

"We can leave now," she said with a smile that caught Lucian's attention—the same one he had witnessed when the world around them had stopped. It was warm and trusting.

She must have those good qualities somewhere inside her heart, right? Lucian thought.

Selena drank her mixture, then threw the goblet behind her. The shattering of it made Lucian jump. Lucian looked at Selena, wondering if she had noticed how skittish he was. She giggled at him. Lucian joined her in laughter. He raised his hand and gently wiped the blood from the corner of Selena's mouth, brushing over her stained, plump lips. Though he was still wary of the discovery of his bride, there was a kindness she showed him. He reaffirmed his grip with her hand as her wings fluttered. They lifted off the ground and soared out the window. The faster Selena flew, the more she glowed, almost making the starry night sky look dull.

Before he knew it, they landed in a lush, green forest. Only a few streams of moonlight pierced through the canopy of trees. Hands still clasped together, Selena guided her husband to a hollowed-out tree. The top looked as if it had broken off, and yet, it still showed life. Dark green moss climbed up the sides of the bark; little toadstools made an upward spiraling staircase. And at the base of the trunk lived a vibrant orange fungus that looked like small mushrooms.

"This was your home?"

"It doesn't look like much, but trust me, it's perfect."

Lucian walked up to the entrance and stepped over the dirt threshold. Fireflies lit up the room. Silk fabrics hung from the branches that intertwined with each other, forming a pitted ceiling. A thick layer of dirt lined the perimeter of the tree and cutouts formed shelving for storage and places to sleep.

"There's a spring not too far that will always provide fresh, clean water for our family, and the forest will supply us with all the food we will need."

Lucian stood, embracing his surroundings. *How could a beautiful place like this be in our world?* he thought. "I couldn't have asked for anything better," he said to Selena.

"It's perfect, isn't it? Right...we must hurry and prepare. Our little bundle can show up anytime now. You should get that protection spell up."

"But you just drank it. How fast do you think having a family is going to take?"

"I know you mortals are used to a drawn out pregnancy, but our incubation period is usually about a day."

"You are full of surprises, aren't you?"

"Guilty. And trust me, you don't know the half of it." Selena smirked as she remembered the very recent death she had just cast out into the world.

Lucian stepped back outside and faced his new home. He outstretched his arms, and with the palms of his hands facing the heavens in order to gather the energy of his surroundings, he then pressed his palms together and took a breath in. With the force of his breath, he pushed his hands forward toward the entrance. As he exhaled, he raised his sturdy arms above his head, then back down to his sides, creating a dome shield covering miles in circumference.

Lucian rejoined Selena inside.

"It's a girl. I can feel her," Selena said as she rocked back and forth, holding her now noticeable belly with one hand and decorating with her gold magic with the other. "She's a strong one. Her energy is kind, yet full of will."

Lucian kneeled down next to Selena and placed one hand on her belly, and listened to the baby. The belly bumped his hand. Lucian looked up at Selena, astounded at how quickly the pregnancy had progressed in such a short time. *Maybe everything will be okay*, he hoped to himself. Lucian stood to hug her, but he couldn't wrap his arms around her wings.

"Oh, let me take care of that." With a snap of her fingers, dust sparked enough to retract her wings back into hiding. She was back in her "human" form. She pulled Lucian in and embraced him.

Weeks flew by, but still no sign of their daughter.

"Her energy is still strong. I'm not worried." Lucian tried to comfort his wife. "Remember, this has never been done—a warlock and a fairy. We have to expect nothing and accept things as they play out."

"I'm not used to not being in control," Selena snapped. She looked at him and realized what she had done. "I'm sorry. I just hope everything is alright."

"I understand. She seems healthy, though. You shouldn't worry. I'll go get some water. Just try to relax."

Selena nodded as he retrieved a bucket and then walked out of the tree.

Lucian finally reached the small river. He plunged the bucket into it. When he picked the full bucket up out of the chilled water, he heard a baby's cries echoing from the depths of the forest. Lucian dropped the bucket of water and ran toward their home. Minutes later, he rushed to Selena's bedside. She was holding their new baby.

"She's here," he gasped, trying to catch his breath. "Are you okay…is she okay?"

For the first time, Selena shed tears. "She's like you, a witch. She isn't a fairy." Selena couldn't decipher if her tears were that of joy or of sadness. The fact she had a daughter was overwhelming as it was, but she had hoped that the child would have followed her bloodline.

"That doesn't matter, Selena. Our love is all she needs."

Selena handed the baby to Lucian. "I wanted a family so that I could pass on my legacy and kingdom to her." Tears continued to fall as she discovered these were sad tears. "I can't stay here and raise her as a mortal. I have a kingdom to run; subjects who need me."

"Selena, she needs you. This is your daughter." He held their child out to her, trying to convince her to stay.

"I don't know how to take care of her. She's nothing like me."

Lucian thought otherwise. He looked into his daughter's eyes, and though they were green rather than the deep purple of Selena's, there was a pureness which Selena had found buried deep that day in the field with the mother and daughter. Surely, there was a love that tethered the baby and Selena now…

Selena transformed into her fairy-self. "I'm sorry, my love, but I cannot stay. I can't raise a witch."

"Selena, how can you leave us?"

"I'll be around. Before I go, I want to give her a gift." Selena picked off a rosebud from her crown, a thin stem and black thorns included, and sprinkled her powder onto it. The flower formed into a butterfly-shaped pendant. Emerald stones, the shade of the baby's eyes, ornately decorated the butterfly's wings. In the center of the insect, three purple garnet stones shone.

"This pendant will protect her from the darkness and allow her to join me in my life for centuries to come. The butterfly is a symbol of reincarnation. Like this delicate creature, my child will never die, but be able to relive her life through the centuries." Selena floated the necklace to her daughter's neck. "Cherish this gift, my love, and know that I am always watching." She kissed her daughter on the forehead, then vanished, leaving nothing but the remnants of gold dust.

"Don't worry, little one, I'll never leave you," her father promised.

A sparrow landed on the windowsill they had carved into their tree. "But of course you will, Lucian. You are mortal. I, however, will indeed never leave her."

Lucian faced the bird. "Did you just talk…Are you…You can transform into anything, can't you?"

"Tweet, Tweet," the sparrow replied, toying with her husband's mind before she flew off.

"I may be mortal, but I'll never abandon you…my sweet Vanessa."

Medieval

"Papa, may I go outside and play?" Vanessa loved being outside, especially during springtime.

"Are your chores done?" Lucian asked as he walked in from outside. He was returning with water from the spring.

"Yes, Papa," Vanessa groaned. She felt like she was always doing chores; she just wanted to play outside.

"What about your lessons?"

"They were easy. I can give and take the candle's flame; I made my small wind funnel; and I tried to make the serum to help with bee stings, but it doesn't seem to work." Vanessa held out her arm. It was red and puffy from where a bee had stung her the previous day.

"Well, let's look at that first, then you may play outside." The father-daughter pair walked over to her nook. "Alright, did you add the lavender?"

"Of course, it is my favorite flower. How could I forget that?"

"Okay. Don't get too brazen with me, child." He was serious but Vanessa saw his smirk. "What about the anemone?"

"Yes."

"And the plantain?"

"Ye…no…oops." Vanessa winced then coyly shrugged her shoulders and smiled faintly with a crinkled nose and embarrassed eyes.

"You mustn't rush, my child. These lessons are important. Try this again. Once you have successfully completed that task, then you may play outside. Take your time. You are strong and smart, Vanessa. You must learn to use those qualities."

"Tap, tap."

Lucian refocused his attention to the faint knocking on the shuddered window. "You may need to use it to protect yourself one day." He knew who, or rather, what was tapping at the window.

Vanessa's reluctant moan reverted Lucian's attention back to his daughter. She hated having to repeat herself on a task. As Lucian rambled on about the importance of focus, Vanessa ignored him and started on the mixture once again.

"Okay, I'm done."

"That was pretty fast. You sure you want to test it out?"

Vanessa shrugged.

"How about I test it first, then if it works, we can heal that bee sting of yours?"

"Sounds good."

They stepped out of their home. Lucian kneeled down and sunk his fingers into the earth. As his fingertips got deeper, he could feel the humid moisture warm him. The dry top layer of soil crumbled aside. Lucian pulled up a seed, and as he stood, it blossomed into a sunflower.

Buzz, Buzz

A single bee appeared and accepted Lucian's offering by sipping the flower's sweet nectar. It then hovered in front of Lucian at eye level. For what seemed like hours, for little Vanessa, the bee and her father stared at each other, as if carrying on a conversation. Finally, the bee calmly landed on Lucian's arm and stung him.

"Vanessa, will you hand me the mixture you made?" Lucian asked as the bee buzzed away.

"Here, Papa."

Lucian dipped his fingers into the goop and spread a thin coat onto his sting. "Well done, child. The sting disappeared almost instantly."

Vanessa jumped up and down, then stopped when the throbbing of her arm reminded her to smear some of the goop onto her own arm. Lucian provided his healing care to his child. Once the swelling went down, Vanessa smiled and rocked back and forth, from heel to toe.

"Go ahead…play, but remember to stay close to home."

"Okay, thank you, Papa."

"Stay close," he reiterated the importance.

"I will." She skipped out into the woods.

Vanessa's favorite spot was a secret from her father, as it was just over the imaginary "safe zone" border. The pond was unusually still, but crystal clear as always.

"Hello? Where is everyone?" No animal was in sight. She scanned across the pond and finally saw her friend. "There you are—by yourself today?" Her feathered friend sat perched on an outstretched limb that hung over the pond.

Chirp, Chirp

The bird hopped a few times as it sang its song. The sparrow launched off the branch and glided just above the mirror-like pond, then landed on Vanessa's shoulder.

Chirp, Chirp

"Hello, birdy. Sorry I was late coming out to play. I had to redo my lesson."

"Vanessa!"

She jumped, but the bird stayed fixed on her shoulder; it didn't waver in the slightest.

"Papa, what are you doing out here?"

"I told you to stay close."

"But I haven't crossed the pond, I promise."

"You shouldn't be out this far. It's too close to the edge." Lucian finally noticed the bird on his daughter's shoulder. "That bird…" he marched right up to Vanessa. "Shoo, Shoo."

"Father, it's my friend." The sparrow bounced around her shoulder, too stubborn to leave.

"Birds are nasty creatures…they carry diseases…and things…shoo I say. Be gone with you, you vile creature."

The bird surrendered and returned to its perch on the limb.

"Come, child." Lucian placed his hand on Vanessa's back, urging her to move toward home. "No more playing with birds, and from now on, you'll stay within our clearing, except to get water from the spring or gather food for our table. Understand?"

"Yes, Papa." Vanessa hung her head as tears welled up. She sniffled to make them disappear so Lucian wouldn't notice. The animals were the only friends she had, and now…they were all gone.

"I'm going out Papa."

"Have you finished your chores and studies?"

"Yes, Papa, there is chamomile tea with a hint of peppermint for your headache."

"Thank—"

Bam

Vanessa slammed the door with a flick of her wrist

"…you. Teenagers…I guess no matter the power, they all go through that stage."

"Yes, they do."

Lucian whipped around. He recognized that sensual, yet heart-piercing voice.

"Selena, what do you want? Why are you here?"

"I needed to spread my wings…pardon…my arms. Being a bird can be quite a compact lifestyle. Anyway, how are you, love?"

"I'm not your love. You left, if you remember."

"Yet here I am."

"Enough trying to be coy and just cut to the chase, Selena. Vanessa will be back soon."

"Not as soon as you think." Selena slowly shook her head from side to side while she watched the gears in Lucian's head grind. His eyes shifted from bitterness towards his wife to concern for his daughter, wondering if Vanessa was in danger.

"She's found a hobby—and, yes…quite a dangerous one."

"Get out of my mind, Selena."

"How could you, as her caring father, let her drift so far away from safety?"

"I tried keeping her close, but she needed the animals; she needed companionship."

"She needed me," Selena tossed in her two cents.

"You are no fool, Selena. Vanessa's want of attention and adventure would be there, with or without you."

"Maybe so, but I did as I promised. I am with her when she needs me." Selena walked around her old home, reminiscing about her first few weeks there as a family with Lucian. She had been happy during that short time. "That's why I'm here, actually. She needs me."

"I'm not listening to anything you want until you tell me where she is."

"Patience, Papa bear, patience. I want to talk to her. She should know me, the real me…not the…oh how did you put it a few years ago…the vile creature."

"Never."

"Suit yourself…keep our daughter safe, won't you? Remember, you only have one life with her. I wouldn't want you to waste it. Let me know when you've changed your mind." And just like that, she flew off.

Lucian did not know what Vanessa had been up to, but he wasn't about to barter with the Dark Queen. He didn't think that Vanessa would be ready to make the right decisions about her mother's gift.

Night fell, and though Vanessa tried to sneak in, she was unsuccessful. As soon as she closed the door behind her, candle light lit the whole treehouse. Lucian was sitting on a mini tree stump which they often used as chairs in the center of the room.

"Papa!"

"Star gazing are we, Vanessa?"

"Um…yes…we'll go with that."

"How about the truth?"

Vanessa squinted her eyes and turned her head, pressing her cheek into her shoulder. "Slaying…dragons…"

When Lucian didn't respond, Vanessa peeked at him. His eyes were glued to hers, as if piercing her with daggers. "Did my daughter just say that she was slaying dragons?" He tried to keep his outward appearance angry, when in his mind, he feared for her safety.

"I keep myself cool by circulating a watery wind tunnel around myself. It works as a shield, too. I've been practicing my sword fighting for years now…alone in the woods. Nothing else for me to do." Vanessa sighed. "I should stop talking. I might as well be digging my own grave."

In an eerily calm, monotone voice, Lucian asked, "How could you keep this from me?"

"How could I tell you? And how did you find out, anyway?"

"I…I'm your father. I know things, but that's besides the point. You can't put yourself in that kind of danger."

"I'm stronger than you think, Papa. I'm helping people not get burned—keeping families alive and safe. I'm doing good and using my powers to help."

Lucian stood, holding up his arm. Vanessa walked up to him and placed her cheek in his cupped hand. "Vanessa, I know you are strong. I felt that before you were even born, but you mean everything to me. I just don't want to see you get hurt."

"I know." Vanessa nestled into the warmth of her father's hand. He meant everything to her, too. She knew how much he loved her, but sometimes she felt he just didn't understand her need to roam free, her urgency for adventure. "Please, let me do this. I'll keep up with my studies and chores, but please…I like the intensity and adventure. It satisfies the urge to run."

Run, Lucian thought. *Did she want to run away? Had she been that unhappy, and if so, had I made her that way?* He hesitated, but gave in. "OK, but… I want to come with you on your next adventure—just to see if there is anything else I can provide to assist in your quest."

Vanessa's eyes sparkled as she looked up at Lucian. "Thank you, Papa. I'll let you know when I go out next. Take note though, it's not for the faint of heart."

"Oh really," Lucian chuckled at his all-grown-up daughter. "I think I can take the heat."

Vanessa embraced Lucian. "I love you, Papa."

"And I you, my butterfly." Lucian pulled back out of the hug and touched her butterfly pendant. His smile faded as memories of what could have been clouded his present.

"What's wrong?"

"Nothing…Want a treat before bed?" His smile returned.

"Silly question, of course I do. I'll grab some berries."

Lucian woke the next morning to an empty house. *She left on her venture without me…I thought we had an understanding. I just wanted her to know that I'm here for her.*

Right before he stood from his bed nook, the door flew open.

"Are you ready for some flames, Papa?"

"Oh, you're here."

"I wouldn't leave you. I said I would take you next time."

Lucian just sat there and thought, *She is finally opening up to me.*

"Let's go, old man. The dragon won't stop causing havoc on its own."

"Oh, right." He stood to get ready for their adventure. "Where did you go then?"

"I went for my morning walk like I always do, then I smelled the burning of a village. We can follow the smoke that rose above the trees on my way back here."

"Well…," Lucian smiled while sitting comfortably on his bed. He took pride in her abilities to track and assess the situation, all while being thrilled with what she was doing. "Let's go get a dragon, then."

The black smoke bellowed over the trees, creating a blanket of smog. The animals were frantic, running every which way, desperate to escape its suffocating hold.

"Where did you get a sword, anyway?" Lucian had never given her a weapon. He didn't really believe in that sort of thing, especially because his kind, as witches, had their hands and powers which are weapons themselves when needed.

"I found it on a walk one morning; a couple of days or so ago."

"It was just lying there?"

"Yes. I had been using a sharpened staff that I whittled, but when I found this, I couldn't pass it up."

"I wonder whose it was."

Lucian wiped his dripping forehead with his shirt just as Vanessa hiked up her shirt a bit. Sweat pooled at the base of her back as they got closer to the fiery flames. The dragon was in sight, but before she advanced, she had to create her shield. Vanessa pulled water from the heather that surrounded the village. She used her hands to mold the water into a shield.

"Stay back, Papa, and watch. I don't want you to get hurt."

"Aww, look who's being the protector now."

Vanessa turned and stomped towards Lucian. Their faces were mere inches away from each other. The crease on the bridge of her nose, between her eyes, let Lucian know how serious his daughter was.

"I'm not playing games. Stay back."

Lucian looked straight into his daughter's eyes, and without faltering said, "I will." He hid behind a small unburnt house, still able to see his daughter in action.

Vanessa raced towards the back of the black and red dragon, but it was as if the beast had eyes in the back of its head. The dragon whipped his head around and shot out a fierce stream of fire. She ducked behind her water shield, which rippled the slightest bit when the fire struck. The dragon lunged at her but missed once again. Before the dragon could retract its neck, Vanessa thrust the sword through the belly of the beast then pulled it out for defense. The dragon stumbled, giving Vanessa the chance to climb onto the back of the agonizing beast and drive the sword into its spine at the base of the neck. Vanessa jumped off. Once she reestablished her footing, she noticed the dragon was swaying towards the house where her father was hiding.

"Look out!"

Vanessa didn't see Lucian move before the dragon fell, crumpling the house into splinters.

"Papa!"

The dust from the crumbling debris added to the haze from the fire, making it hard for her to find her way to where Lucian had stood. She absorbed some of the charred flames into her shield to make her path clearer.

She heard coughing.

"Papa?"

"It's alright," he coughed again, "I'm alright, my butterfly."

She reached out her hand toward his voice and finally felt Lucian's hand grab her fingertips.

"Someone, or something, pushed me aside."

The black air finally started to clear, then a reflection shined into Vanessa's eyes. She raised her sword, keeping Lucian sheltered behind her.

"Who's there?"

"I mean you no harm. My name is Tristan, Sir Tristan. I'm a knight of King Edward III, from Windsor castle."

Vanessa lowered her weapon.

"Nice sword," the stranger said.

"Thank you," Vanessa admired its bloody gleam in the sun.

"It's mine," Tristan laughed. "I got thrown from my horse, and my sword took a journey of its own."

"And then I found it in the woods."

"I tracked you by your footprints, going downwind, but then I saw you running with the sword towards the dragon. I figured I could offer my assistance, though in hindsight, with you having my sword, I suppose there wasn't much I could have helped with. You took care of the dragon, so I swooped in to help…"

"Lucian." Vanessa's father came around her and extended his hand to greet the knight. "And this is my daughter, Vanessa. You saved my life, and for that, I am forever in your debt."

"It is my duty. Think nothing of it."

After some awkward silence, with a dead dragon just a few feet from them, Lucian spoke up, "Well, won't you let us feed you before you set off on your journey back to Windsor?"

"I appreciate your hospitality. Thank you."

Lucian pulled back behind Tristan and Vanessa on their way back home. *I'm sure the animals were superb listeners, but at least now she can have a two-way conversation*, Lucian thought. He laughed at himself as he continued, this time out loud, "And yet, here I am having a two-way conversation with myself."

The new friends looked back at Lucian, questioning his sanity.

"Carry on," he cleared his throat, embarrassed at being caught, "I'm just lost in my thoughts." He waved his hands, directing them to continue the walk home.

The trio sat at the table. They broke bread together, sipped homemade blackberry mead, and talked until the wee hours of the morning.

"I best be setting off." Tristan bowed with gratitude.

"Won't you stay for a while?" Vanessa had just met another human, she didn't want him to rush off so soon.

"We get little rest time as knights, but I suppose since I was early on my way back to Windsor, another day's delay wouldn't hurt."

"Oh good, Papa. Do you mind if I show him around?"

"You can forget chores today, but please don't slack on your studies. They are there to guide and protect you. Since you have picked up slaying dragons, it is more important than ever…no matter the distraction." He eyed Tristan, then quickly added, "My apologies."

Tristan nodded his understanding.

"Yes, Papa, I'll do them tonight. I don't want to run out of daylight."

Lucian tossed her an eyeroll of disappointment. Studies should always come first in his eyes, but the nagging voice of a particular sparrow pressured for some leniency.

"How do you pull magic from around you?"

"What do you mean?"

"The only magic I've witnessed is that of a mystical object. I have never seen a human pull resources from around them, thus creating magic."

"Well, think of it as an exchange. In order for one to use magic, one must offer a sacrifice of some sort. For instance, my water shield I form when I fight draws the water from the heather—the flowers, stem, and soil. The action of me taking that water caused death to the flower as a consequence."

"That's fascinating. I just have—" Tristan looked down at the sword Vanessa had secured to her hip. He playfully nudged her. "Well, I should say I 'had' a sword."

"Being cooped up day after day practicing spells is hardly fascinating. You get to go on adventures, fight in battles, fight dragons—"

"You fight dragons, or was that a figment of my imagination?"

Vanessa giggled, nudging him back. "It was me, but until just a few days ago, it was a secret from my father. If it were up to him, I'd never go outside."

"He's just trying to protect you."

"I know, but sometimes it's too constricting. Don't get me wrong, I love him dearly. I'd do anything for him, but I just need some air."

The friends talked all day. Vanessa even shared her special spot by the pond.

"This is breathtaking." Tristan saw the picturesque view. The still, yet whimsical mist of the pond triggered his thoughts, which he shared with Vanessa. "This water, this place…it reminds me of the story about the Lady in the Lake."

Vanessa tilted her head.

"You know the story of King Arthur and the siren, Nimue?"

She shook her head.

"Well, I won't bore you with all the details. They might bore you since you slay dragons and all. But Nimue was known to be an enchantress dwelling under a most magical lake. She ended up giving King Arthur the most mystical sword named Excalibur."

"Where is the sword now?"

"Why, looking for a replacement?" He shot a glance at her with the cheekiest of smirks.

Vanessa giggled and leaned into him.

"Before the King died, he tossed it back into the same lake from where he had received it."

"No one's gone after it?"

"Oh, many have tried, and many have failed. Only one that I know of came back in one piece. He said it was jammed in a boulder at the bottom of the lake. No matter how hard he pulled, the thing wouldn't budge."

"What happened to the others?"

"I'm assuming their greed got hold of them and ended up drowning. They just couldn't let go."

"Have you thought about giving it a go?"

"I have…" Tristan nodded slowly as his gaze hovered over the still lake.

Vanessa was expecting the conversation to continue, but she stood quietly, watching as he daydreamed of the possibility. After some time, they sat at the edge of the pond, simply enjoying the companionship of one another.

Across the way sat the little sparrow. She watched the pair; the thought of Vanessa with someone other than her left a foul taste in her mouth. It could have been the worm she had eaten that morning, but she doubted it. The sparrow bounced and ruffled her feathers. *After all this time of being her confidante, her advisor, her friend—had she forgotten all about me? Was this boy going to replace me?* The bird continued to chirp and flounce about, then she decided she had had enough, and flew off.

Night was falling; the two headed back to the treehouse.

"You might as well stay the night…rest up before heading home."

"Thank you. I think I shall."

They opened the door and greeted Lucian.

"Hello, Papa."

"Sir." Tristan nodded.

"Hello, kids. Did you enjoy your day?"

"It was lovely," Tristan acknowledged as he smiled at his new friends.

"I've offered for him to stay, if that's alright, Papa."

"Of course, you are our guest."

"Much obliged."

After staying up the previous night and their adventures of the day, they all slept peacefully that night.

The next morning, Vanessa woke up coughing. She opened her eyes, then shut them as embers from a close-by fire burned them.

"Papa…Tristan…"

"We're okay…try to find the door."

Vanessa took in a breath as best as she could, and blew a circle around her, attempting to clear a path. She shuffled around and found the door, but when she opened it, it didn't seem to help clear the air much. More smoke just pushed its way in. Vanessa bent down. Though not crystal clear, it was easier to see, and the heat wasn't as stifling. She crawled over to her hidden stash of flowers. Vanessa had kept them there for her adventures, a secret from Lucian. She found some pansies, thankfully with a bubbled dew resting on its petals. Vanessa continued her search for a toadstool. Once found, she crushed the two objects into her hands, then threw it up into the air. When the mixture fell to the ground, it was as if gravity no longer worked. Droplets kissed the dry dirt, then floated into the air. Rain fell within seconds, and within a few moments, as the ash began to clear, Vanessa could finally see the dragon. It was right on top of them.

Vanessa yelled at the two men standing at the tree stump, "You must leave! Find shelter by the pond."

"We aren't leaving you." Lucian had no plans to abandon his daughter.

"Where's the sword?" Tristan looked around. He saw it leaning up against the open tree-trunk's door frame. "Vanessa, catch."

Vanessa, just a few feet forward of the house and the boys, was in the perfect spot; right under the dragon's belly. She caught the sword, but by the time she looked up to strike, the dragon had noticed them there, and had moved its position. Just then, something flew in front of her head. She tracked it to the house to where Tristan was. It seemed hysterical as it attacked his face.

The sparrow…what is it doing here? Vanessa didn't know how to prioritize. *Sure, the bird seemed harmless, especially compared to the other winged-thing that blew fire. But why was it attacking Tristan?*

The skies opened up, and the slow trickle of rain was now a steady flow flooding the fields.

This is good, Vanessa attempted to reassure herself amid the chaos. She had to make a choice. Where was she needed the most? *A dragon, which can hurt the masses, must outweigh a bird attacking a friend.* Wincing at the decision, she searched for a better position on the dragon since it changed its course, but she kept looking back at Tristan. Blood started dripping from Tristan's head.

"Vanessa, stay focused." She heard her father yelling, not exactly sure where he was.

"Papa, are you hurt?"

"Don't worry about me. Focus. You must focus."

She looked back at Tristan. He was on his knees, screaming in pain as the irate bird continued to scratch and peck at her new friend.

Vanessa heard a thud. The dragon jumped toward a figure.

"Papa! No! Over here!" Vanessa yelled, catching the scaly beast's attention, hoping to divert it from her father.

It worked. The dragon focused on Vanessa. It stomped towards her, the tail swinging right over Tristan's head.

"Oh, no! Tristin!" Blood had pooled at his knees. Vanessa started running towards him.

"Vanessa!" Lucian noticed the dragon had made his daughter its newest target. Nothing was going to break its focus on her.

Sadly, Vanessa's mind was not on the dragon, but on her friend, who was leaving just as soon as he had entered her life. Her father's warning failed to reach her. The dragon snapped at her. She turned around and realized the close call when she was pushed by the dragon's breath. Before she could rear back her sword, it snapped again, this time catching her leg. She screamed as she collapsed to the ground, then looked to see how bad the wound was. Her leg was gone.

Vanessa was splayed out, paralyzed and uncertain of her next move. She looked around her and realized the rain had stopped. She saw her new friend bleeding out, her father now the dragon's new target, and she, herself, could not help them.

Fire erupted from the dragon. Her world got darker…cloudier. She wasn't sure if it was from the fires that had reignited since the rain had stopped, or if it was the loss of blood. Vanessa tried to think back to the thousands of lessons Papa had drilled into her head, but her mind was murky; nothing stayed steady enough for her weak mind to focus on. It was harder for her to keep her eyelids open. Her body was heavy. She could feel it sinking into the soil, as if sinking right into a grave. Vanessa heard her last heartbeat, then closed her eyes.

Chirp

"Vanessa," Selena said as she flew over to her daughter's side while transforming from bird to queen. She glided down as a swan would to a lake, wings shifting into arms and tucked talons reaching out to feet. "Vanessa", Selena tried again, but it was too late. Vanessa was gone from this life. Selena's attention quickly turned to the dragon, watching to see where he was heading.

Selena left her daughter to follow the dragon and search for Lucian. "Lucian," she cried out into the woods. Lucian jumped at the sound of Selena's voice, which only raised the alarm for the dragon to pursue him. The dragon lunged at Lucian, picking him up by his hair and tossed him up into the air. But before Lucian could fall into the belly of the beast, Selena clapped her hands with enough force that her gold glitter created a wave. When the wave slammed into the dragon, it disappeared.

"This was not the plan, my pet. It is time for you to leave us now." Selena only conjured the dragon as an escape for Vanessa. It was time she had with her daughter although Selena didn't see Vanessa's death happening so soon.

Lucian screamed as he descended towards the ground.

"Oh, stop your whining," Selena scolded. She rose off the ground and held out her arms to catch Lucian.

"Get off me, Selena." He pushed her away. Out of spite, Selena dropped him to the ground.

Lucian scrambled towards Vanessa, who lay in a bed of ash and blood. "Oh no. No, no… My sweet butterfly." He turned to face his ex. "How could you do this? I should have known better; now that I think about it, this whole thing reeks of your magic. All of this was nothing but a selfish ploy to have time with a daughter you wanted nothing to do with."

"I had it under control…"

"Do you not see our dead daughter?" He wiped the drenched hair off Vanessa's face and placed her hands on her chest.

"Lucian, I warned you." She stood with her chin and lips resting on her fingers minus her index finger, which she was using to tap on her cheek. "You kept her on a tight leash and pushed her away. You had one chance with her and you blew it."

"How dare you put this on me! You created this mess—the dragon, the distraction with her first friend…you did this, Selena."

"I was her friend. I will not let some boy take that from me."

"You let our daughter die because you were jealous?!" Lucian stood up with his palms facing the sky.

"What…you're going to kill me, husband?"

Lucian didn't answer. He raised his hands above his head and clapped them together.

"Lucian, stop this nonsense. I don't want to hurt you."

"You don't even seem like you've lost a daughter. I know you'll see her in years to come, but how can you live with yourself, knowing that you caused this?"

"I'll have time to make it right. But Lucian, you know as well as I do that your magic won't hurt me. Just take your anger out on something else and live the rest of your life. I love you, my dear. You gave me such a priceless gift. Vanessa is a beauty, outside and in her soul."

Lucian brought his hands down, pressing his palms together. He shook as he glared at Selena. Any love he once had was now buried so deep in his heart, never to resurface.

"Lucian, no."

He went to push his hands forward towards her.

Before he stretched his arms out to their fullest extent, Selena snapped her glittered fingers. Lucian collapsed to the ground next to Vanessa's body. Selena bent down to caress his face. A tear or two dropped onto his forehead.

"You left me no choice, Lucian. I am sorry it had to end this way. Rest well, my love."

Selena fluttered to her daughter and hovered. She then blew a kiss to Vanessa, scattering her dust, and Vanessa disappeared.

"Until next time."

Renaissance

Marcus shuffled up the creaky steps to his little loft, which resided above a butcher's shop. Though the smell wasn't pleasant, the view was transcendent. Therefore, Marcus made it his home and inspiration for the majority of his paintings. At the top of the first flight of steps, he heard noises coming from above. They didn't sound desperate; nonetheless, it wasn't a typical sound for him to hear coming from his home. He proceeded up the next flight with more urgency than when he had begun.

Slightly out of breath, he reached his door. There was a basket sitting in front of the tattered mat placed before his threshold. The blanket that was bundled up inside the basket was moving. Marcus peered into it.

"Why…it's a baby. What are you doing out here? Where do you belong?" He reached down and picked up the baby girl. A necklace hung from her neck; the pendant was that of a butterfly. "I will raise you as my child, provide you with care and love, and share the beauty of the arts. I shall call you…Vanessa."

"Father, did something bad happen when I was a baby?"

"No, not that I can recollect. Why do you ask, my child?"

"I have this big scar around my leg." Vanessa raised her dress just above her knee to show her father the jagged, raised white mark that encircled her leg.

"Come sit with me, my dear." Marcus motioned for her to join him in the kitchen. He picked up Vanessa and sat her on his lap.

"You were a gift. I found you when you were really little. Blankets wrapped around you, keeping you warm and cozy. The only thing you came with was your butterfly necklace."

"This one?" Vanessa pulled the pendant out from under her dress.

"The same." He smiled.

"So, what about this mark?" She raised her dress once more and touched the scar.

"I'm not sure, you…"

Marcus went on explaining that she had it when he had found her. However, Vanessa flashed back. She remembered a man. He struggled, making little Vanessa's heart ache. "Lucian…Papa." The name bounced around in her memories. He had been her father, her real father. She looked around to see what he was cowering away from.

"Dragon," she said out loud, not meaning to.

"What?" Marcus wasn't sure if he heard her correctly.

"Just daydreaming. I think." In all honesty, Vanessa didn't quite understand what she had just seen. She supposed it could have been as simple as a dream, but it felt too tangible. The pain cut too deep. Vanessa looked down at her scar again. It was then that she knew she had seen another life. As if someone had planted a flip book of her most treasured moments in her head. Lucian, her friend, a sparrow, and a dragon.

"Father?" Vanessa rubbed her necklace absentmindedly.

"Yes?"

"What happens after you die?"

Marcus' eyes widened, looking like that of an owl. He opened his mouth but no words came out.

"Nevermind. Can we paint?" She jumped off Marcus' lap and headed to the other side of the small loft.

"I'll be right there. I'll get us some snacks." Marcus was used to her short attention spans, and this time, he was beyond grateful for the change of subject.

"Deliziosa! What are we having?"

"Some berries and Polenta e Osei."

Vanessa jumped up and down, giddy with delight for the chocolatey-cream cake.

"Alright, dear child," he said as he walked in with the tray of desserts. "What are we painting today?"

Marcus turned to face her canvas, which showed a still, crystal clear pond with the sky reflecting off the water. "This one again?" He tilted his head with a crooked smile. "You have quite the imagination. Where do you see these beautiful places?"

"My dreams." Vanessa continued to paint though now she knew that those dreams had been hints of her past life.

"You're such a good little artist."

"Thank you, Father." She took her paintbrush and smacked the bristles on Marcus' nose.

"Paint fight," Marcus shouted as he picked up the bowl holding the paints and flung it at Vanessa. "What shall you use as your ammunition now?" he playfully taunted.

Vanessa remembered what Lucian had once taught her. All berries had different colors. He had shown her that so she could recognize them and learn which ones to put in the mixtures she created for her studies.

She smiled and looked at Marcus from the corner of her eye. Vanessa grabbed the plate of berries and smashed them into his clean muslin shirt. The colors were vibrant against the crisp white, and an idea struck Vanessa's mind.

"Father, may I have some more berries?"

"I think my shirt has enough color," Marcus said as he pulled his shirt out a bit from his body and saw the beautiful purples and reds.

"No, silly, I have an idea."

"Alright, what kind would you like?"

"Strawberry per favore."

Marcus raised his eyebrows, unsure if he should keep his guard up, or if this was just another one of his daughter's artsy moments. He rinsed the strawberries, then walked over to hand Vanessa the bowl. She was staring at her canvas. She turned the paintbrush around and used the end to crush the strawberries. Once the juices filled the bottom of the bowl, she dipped the brush into the red berry, touched the canvas, and watched as it soaked up the color. It was poetic; the perfect color for her autumn trees in the pond scene.

"Bellissima, figlia mia! Dream big, my child."

Vanessa walked the pathway to the market, watching the river dance in the warm, early sun.

"Good morning, my friend," she greeted a bird as it landed on her shoulder. "How are you doing?"

Chirp, Chirp. It nestled into her cheek.

"Glad to hear it."

The two strode on, enjoying the smells and colors of the fall day.

"You know," Vanessa pondered her feathered company, "I had a friend like you once, a lifetime ago. It was all I had until the end. I found a friend like me…you know…human. The bird reacted poorly to the new bond. I lost everything that day…family and friends." Vanessa fixated on a couple of little birds in the street, playing about and bouncing around.

Chirp.

Vanessa then lowered her gaze, looking at people's feet as they passed her by. "I miss my Papa. I know Marcus, who has been a noble father…and I would never dream of calling him anything other than my father because he has raised me too…but, I miss my Papa."

Chirp.

"You're right. I just have to press forward. I wonder how I came to be alive again. Does everyone come back after they die?"

Chirp. The sparrow twitched its feathers as if shrugging its shoulders.

"I don't know either. Anyway, don't be like the last sparrow. Be a better friend, okay?"

Chirp, Chirp.

"Good, now let's find some flowers for our walk and some berries for our canvas."

"I'm back, Father."

"I'm in here..working on a piece. Find some good things at the market?"

"I think so. I might go back with some of my art; see if I can sell any."

"Good luck with that."

Vanessa could hear the snarkiness in his tone.

"Why do you say that?"

"No offense, my dear, but you are a woman. Whether a masterpiece or trash, no one will buy it."

"I love my work. And there isn't any harm in trying."

"Your work is beautifully…unique. And you're right, it won't hurt anything, but maybe your heart."

"I'll take my chances." Vanessa grabbed one of her paintings of the pond, one of the dragon, and one of her old tree home, then stormed out down the stairs. *Just because I paint from a different world doesn't mean people won't like it*, she gruffed to herself.

She set up next to the flower shop. The smells pleasantly overwhelmed her, reminding her of her past country home. A cool breeze attempted to use her pictures as sails, but Vanessa's strength drew them back into her body. Once the breeze died down, she set up shop, propping the scenes against a lamppost and her knees as she sat on a small wooden stool.

Vanessa greeted those who stopped by, but they only responded with whispers and head shaking.

"Was Father right?" she asked her feathered friend who had made itself comfortable on the pond painting.

By the end of the day, she'd had enough of the rejection, but she was not about to go back home and let her father know he was right.

Instead, Vanessa grabbed her bag that was filled from her earlier market run. She needed to clear her head. She wrapped herself tighter with her shawl as she walked to the tree line and disappeared into the woods.

Silence.

Stillness.

Yet nature was bustling about. Critters busied themselves by filling their bellies and warming their homes for the arrival of snow that would soon be upon them. She stood in the middle of a clearing of trees. As she closed her eyes and spread her arms, letting the shawl drape on her arms like wings, she heard the winds speak to her in their hushed whispers. Doubt and her Father's harsh words blew out of her mind.

Chirp.

"It is lovely, isn't it?" Her sparrow was surfing the wind as its currents ebbed and flowed like the ocean.

Chirp, Chirp.

"Where are you going?" The sparrow left in one direction, then came back, only to repeat its path again. "Do you want to show me something?" Vanessa chased after it. A little way down a hill, she heard a voice.

"I don't know what I'm doing. Nowhere to go…why did I leave?" It was a girl. A child, actually, spinning in circles as if trying to figure out which way to go. Her clothes were tattered and her hair knotted. Dark circles framed her glassy eyes, and her skin almost hung on her frame.

"Ciao?"

The girl picked up a stick and faced Vanessa. The girl's hand shook. "Who are you? What do you want?"

"I will not hurt you…I promise. My name is Vanessa."

"I'm Cristina," she said, still shaking the stick that was pointed at Vanessa.

"Hello, Cristina. What are you doing out here all alone?"

"I had to get away." The girl started lowering the stick as she looked behind her. A crunch of a leaf put the girl back on guard. She raised the stick again and cried. "I'm not going back."

"It's okay Cristina, I will not harm you or put you in any danger."

The stick fell out of the girl's hand as she fell to a crumple on the ground.

Vanessa wanted to rush to her side. Someone had clearly abused her in some sort of way, but Vanessa slowly walked over to Cristina so as to not startle the child. Vanessa removed her wrap, then placed it around the girl, and kneeled down next to her.

"What's your story, Cristina?"

In-between sniffles, the girl responded, "It's too sad to tell."

"Okay, well, tell me a story or a dream…anything you wish."

A small smile broke Cristina's sadness. "I have this dream where I'm dancing in a grassy meadow. Flowers of all sorts and colors shine in the bright sun. I see people in the distance, so I run towards them, thinking they are friendly…"

"Sounds perfect. Then what happens?"

"It's my parents." The frown resurfaced. "I stop running to them when I see their faces. Their smiles are fake. I can tell. They look like puppet faces. They don't love me."

"I'm sure that's not true."

Cristina stood. "I knew you would be on their side."

"No, no." Vanessa grabbed her hand, making the scared girl jump. "Mi dispiace, I'm sorry. I am here to listen."

Cristina sat back down, wrapping the shawl around her knees as she hugged them into her chest. "They don't love me."

They sat in the woods, listening to the world around them. Vanessa didn't press Cristina. She waited, letting Cristina decide when she wanted to continue her story.

Cristina scooted towards Vanessa, who welcomed her into her arms. Vanessa noticed she was shivering. *How long has she been out here?* Vanessa wondered.

After a while, Cristina stopped shaking and sat up. "My mother left years ago; I only have a few memories of her. The ones I have were great. But then I'm left with the question of why she would leave me." Cristina took a deep breath in and quietly said, "Once she left, my father…" She rolled up her sleeves. "He got out of control with drinking and took his anger out on me."

Bruises covered Christina's arms along with a gash which looked infected.

"Oh, Cristina." Vanessa took her arm with care, then looked through her bag from the market. She grabbed lavender and sweet pea from her satchel, then looked around to find… "Yes, cypress." Vanessa crushed everything up in her hands. "Now I just need some water."

"There is a stream just a little farther into the woods." Cristina and Vanessa walked together with the sparrow trailing just behind them.

Vanessa scooped up some water with her free hand then slowly sprinkled the flower dustings into it, forming a watery, elegant smelling liquid.

"May I have your arm?"

Cristina offered it to Vanessa without hesitation. A trust had formed between the two. Vanessa poured the concoction into the infected wound. Vanessa warmed her hands by rubbing them together, then placed the heated energy on Cristina's arm.

The pain dissipated and so did the blacked veins that stemmed outwards from the old wound.

"How did you do that?" Cristina touched her fresh skin.

"I will show you everything. No one deserves the life you have had to endure. The woods can be your new home, and I can teach you how to make a life for yourself out here."

"Home…" Cristina looked down at a cluster of small, orange mushroom-like foliage. "It wasn't always bad, you know. We were once a happy family. Home used to be a place that I felt safe in." She brushed a tear from her cheek. "I suppose you are right, though. I don't deserve to be hurt. Home is where you make it, right? I would love for you to teach me how to be on my own."

"Home," Vanessa thought. "I think you have helped me as much as I have helped you, Cristina," Vanessa said, then smiled at her young apprentice.

"Now, the first lesson is to remember one important thing. My Papa taught me this long ago. Balance is a necessity in our world. Good and evil coexist because of this balance. For example, if I take the vibrant color of this fungus…" Vanessa hovered her hands over the colony that Cristina was just looking at. "and transfer the color to something lacking in pigment, like my dress…" A pinpoint of orange quickly scattered across the fabric like arteries carrying blood from the heart.

"That is so pretty. How wonderful."

"But now look at the mushrooms."

"They are gray and sickly."

Vanessa nodded. "Yes. A pretty mushroom is so much more than a pretty mushroom. Just like you are so much more than just a pretty girl. Everything has an energy or life source. The mushroom had something to offer: its color, its water, its beauty. If you accept this offering, the life force in the object you use could die. You must weigh the reward with its potential consequence."

"I think I understand." Cristina picked up the shriveled mushroom. "Can you fix it?"

"Yes, but bringing things back from death also has a cost. Most times, the cost is usually too high to pay."

Vanessa listened to the words that just came out of her mouth. She wondered, *Does this mean that this second life of mine is causing death somewhere else? Or was it normal for people to be reborn life after life?*

She put her focus back onto Cristina, who was holding the mushroom up to Vanessa's orange stained dress. The thin streams retreated to the mushroom, bringing the vibrant life back to its shell. Cristina smiled at the restored fungus.

"Now, how is it supposed to sustain the life that you gave back? It is no longer rooted in the soil. Its stem no longer has a nutrient-rich environment from which to drink."

"I hadn't thought of that."

"You must. The new life is now shortened. It now suffers as it struggles to survive."

Cristina cried again.

"It's alright. We can give it safe passage by accepting its gifts again." Vanessa moved Cristina's hand to her dress.

The orange jumped from the mushroom onto the girl's dress. A smile returned to Cristina's innocent face. She twirled with delight. "Now I will always have a part of the mushroom."

Vanessa responded with a smile.

Cristina's passion and understanding of nature and the magic it offered flourished quickly over the next couple of weeks they shared. Vanessa thought her prodigy had learned what she needed in order to survive, plus more to help guide her through whatever may come her way.

Vanessa hugged Cristina and said, "You have taught me what home feels like, and now that you have made one for yourself, I must return to mine. I miss it, and I have some business to attend to. Now, thanks to you, I feel fairly certain I may succeed in my endeavors with little hardship."

"I can't thank you enough, Vanessa, for your wise words and friendship. Shall I stop in to visit soon?"

"Please do. I insist."

With a bittersweet farewell, Vanessa journeyed back home.

Vanessa nudged the cracked open door to her loft.

"You're back," Marcus mumbled.

"Yes, I am. Good to be home. How have you been?"

Vanessa turned the corner to see Marcus slouching in his chair. Marcus raised his arm, a cup clenched in his hand; the alcohol sloshed about. "I've been doing just as well as you have, I'd imagine," he hiccupped.

"What do you mean?"

"You have been gone for some time now. I'm assuming that is due to you not wanting to admit to your failure. I told you it wouldn't work out…didn't I?" His drunken stupor was not becoming of the father she knew.

"Yes," Vanessa fessed up boldly. "However," she raised her voice to overpower his laughter, "I know how to turn my luck around."

"Do you know?" He took another drink, leaning all the way back to finish the last desperate drop. "And how is that, my dear?"

"You'll just have to wait and see, I suppose. It's my business, anyway. From the sounds of it, you should be reflecting on how you will fix your failure." Vanessa was furious at her father's unsupportive words.

Marcus raised his cup to his sloppy lips again.

"You drank it all," Vanessa spat.

He lowered the empty cup once he realized she was right. They stared at each other for a second or two. Marcus reared his arm back with the cup in hand, as if he was going to throw it. But he pulled back too far and ended up falling out of his chair. The cup bounced off his forehead. The drunkard passed out, not by the light-weighted cup, but by alcohol.

"Sleep it off, Marcus." She had never called him by anything other than "Father" until this point. It didn't feel right putting him in the same category as Lucian. She stepped over Marcus' leg and headed to her room.

Vanessa overlooked the river that flowed just outside her window. The colors of the buildings reflected off of the dancing pool, which gave it a mosaic look. It was as if Vanessa was looking at her surroundings for the very first time. This was her current home, not the forest from her past. Her neighbors were her target audience for her paintings. They didn't want to see a dream world. They wanted to see their world, maybe in a different light. Vanessa decided, "I think it is time to show these people the beauty of their world."

Vanessa studied her window view—the colors, the life, the sounds. She wanted to capture the very essence of her world, spending days on end playing with different times of day and watching how the colors changed the mood of her paintings.

After a few weeks, she had finished a collection of paintings. The common theme being the river that was loved by all in her community. She gathered all of her paintings and supplies and headed down to the market for another day at selling her work.

This time, the townspeople greeted and conversed with Vanessa. Before the sun had set, there wasn't a painting left.

Vanessa whistled as she entered her home that evening.

"I see you have been busy." Marcus was in her room, viewing the painting that hadn't dried in time to take with her that day. "You have certainly changed your strokes…do you really think that a change of scenery will help you sell them? Last I knew, you are still a woman."

"Interesting…"

"What?"

"It is true. I am indeed a woman. But not all people are as derogatory as you are. They simply don't care who they buy beauty from. In fact, Marcus…" she paused, feeling relieved at the fact that she no longer felt she had to call him by a patriarchal name.

Marcus raised his eyebrows at the confidence of his name escaping her mouth.

"I just returned from a full day at the market, and I came back empty-handed."

Marcus babbled, "But…how…?"

"I don't give up, Marcus. You taught me that. Although it looks as if you need to heed your own words. You don't even try to paint anymore. You've taken up the hobby of drinking; that is abundantly clear." Vanessa pinched her nose as his gaping mouth was spilling a sour odor. "Now, if you don't mind, these paintings should be dry by morning. I should sleep, so I am properly refreshed."

Marcus glared at Vanessa's back as she turned, lightly checking on her paintings. Then he backed out of the room. He went back to his chair, this time with no drink…lost in deep thought.

"I had a splendid day, sparrow. When you left for lunch, people stopped and expressed the beauty of your feathers in my paintings. You have been so influential in my life…lives…I figured I'd feature you in my painting. It's like my signature. Hope you don't mind?"

Chirp

"Good." Vanessa rubbed the little bird's head with her finger. "Your feathers are so pretty. They have a faint glow of purple. I used blackberries and a pinch of wine for their color. Will you stay with me tomorrow? I'm sure people would love to compare the paintings with my real muse."

Chirp

"Until tomorrow then. Let's get some shuteye."

That night, the moon shone its full light into Vanessa's room. A small burst of gold glitter erupted in the room, giving the moon a halo. Selena stretched out her aching arms. She had been a sparrow for a while now. She fluttered her fairy wings to her daughter's bedside.

"I wish I could talk to you, my sweet child, but I promised your father I wouldn't. He was right. It isn't the right time. I am so proud of you. You are kind, strong, and so beautiful."

Selena dusted her daughter's head with her magical dust. "I hope you hear me. It is important. Heed my warning, my dear butterfly. I fear your next death seems to be nigh. Please look out for the shadows that lurk. Darkness looms around your artwork." Selena bent down and kissed Vanessa's forehead then flew out the window, casting a shadow on her bedsheets.

Once the moon sank into its slumber, Vanessa woke and eagerly got ready for her day. She walked out, expecting to see Marcus in his usual spot, but he wasn't in the loft at all—not that she really cared anymore—so she thought nothing of it and headed downstairs.

Her sparrow met her in the busy street. It settled on Vanessa's shoulder and they headed off down the road. When they reached Vanessa's normal spot by the flower shop, a crowd greeted her.

"Hello. Hello," she greeted as she made her way through. As soon as she set up her works of art, a bidding war broke out. Word had traveled overnight about her paintings. All the day's pieces had vanished by the time the sun was at its peak, but her audience didn't mind waiting for her to create more. Vanessa took orders for them.

Vanessa's spirits were high. She felt appreciated and accomplished. Many of her new friends walked with her back to her home that night, conversing the whole time. They all said their goodbyes, then Vanessa headed up to her home, already coming up with ideas of new scenes to paint. The ever-watchful sparrow stayed outside, but Vanessa expected to meet up with her at her windowsill.

Upon entry to the building, Vanessa hadn't noticed that the butcher had closed early. The door to her loft was open…not how she had left it.

"Marcus?" She pushed the door open, figuring he had forgotten to close the door in another drunken stupor.

Besides the creek of the hinges, there was no response. "I sold out today…again."

She recalled a voice from a dream…but the memory was too late. The loft door slammed shut behind her. Before she could find a light source, Vanessa ran to her room, but she wasn't able to close her door in time. Something pushed against, forcing her to the floor.

"Who are you?" Vanessa scooted backwards. "What do you want from me?"

Still no response from the stranger. She heard tapping on the window.

"Must be Sparrow," Vanessa concluded. She crawled quietly, using the darkness to her favor. She made it to the window. The moonlight beamed into the room, providing enough light to see the attacker's lower body. Blood stained the white fabric.

"The butcher? Why are you doing this?"

Then a voice reverberated in her chest. But it wasn't the butcher. It was Marcus. "This is a man's world…You were told, but failed to listen. Your vile mouth should have kept its harsh words towards me silent."

"Marcus? But you raised me as your own. How could you?"

Marcus stepped out from the dark corner of the room, making the moon form a mask around his eyes. The butcher was now behind her, holding what she could only imagine as a knife to her back.

"It is one thing to be a father to an obedient daughter, but I have worked my whole life for a break like you recently lucked into. I refuse to be known as the 'Father to a Master Artist'…and a woman, at that! Yes, I raised you. I should have implemented a certain discipline in you rather than encourage such an imagination. I was foolish to underestimate you, that I'll admit. But you have basked in your glory long enough. It is my turn."

With a stiff, unremorseful nod from Marcus, the butcher smoothly pressed the knife into Vanessa's back, crippling her to the floor, her cheek pressed against the splintered wood. The two men waited for Vanessa to bleed out. Marcus needed assurance. Vanessa could still hear the sparrow pecking at the glass and the constant chirping.

Knock, Knock

The two men slipped back into the darkness, hoping the visitor would just leave, but the door opened. A candle flickered. Vanessa tried to give a warning to the visitor, but couldn't move. She was paralyzed, and the pain had sealed her lips. She could feel the warmth seep out of her body. Tears slowly trickled down her face as she knew her life was once again coming to an end. She didn't want people to see her cry, but this time, she could not wipe them away. The flame and its owner drew closer.

"Cristina?" Vanessa forced herself to speak. Her friend was in grave danger.

"Oh, Vanessa," Cristina choked up in tears. "What happened?"

Cristina saw Vanessa struggle for words. She placed her hand on her shoulder blade, attempting to comfort her dying mentor.

"Run," Vanessa coughed out blood, as she was finally able to give her friend some kind of warning. Cristina looked into Vanessa's eyes and sensed the urgency of her single word. Vanessa felt the floor vibrate as the hidden men walked towards the two girls.

Cristina teared up. She kissed Vanessa on the forehead.

"Run," Vanessa mouthed.

Cristina shot up, ducking under the butcher's arm, and ran for the door.

Vanessa watched as her friend left the loft. She hoped Cristina made it out of death's way. Vanessa was cold now and drifted deeper and deeper into the darkness.

The sparrow saw the light fade from her daughter. Selena changed out of her bird confines, then went around to the front of the building and waited up against the wall. Once she saw Cristina run out towards her wooded home, Selena jumped in front of the entrance, blocking the butcher and Marcus.

"Hello, boys."

"Get out of the way," Marcus said as he tried to push through Selena.

"I don't think that's going to happen." Selena shook her head and lightly clicked her tongue to the roof of her mouth, which caused a shameful sound. "You have already killed my daughter. I will not let you kill her friend. I made that mistake already."

"Get out of our way, woman." Marcus slapped Selena across the face.

Selena turned her head back and looked at the chuckling men. Then she extended her arms and grabbed their throats, raising them up from the last step they had been standing on. "That wasn't very nice."

"What…"

"You don't want to know what I am. You should ask what I'm going to do with you two. Hmm…having watched you spiral out of control, I think death would be an easy out for you. I have just the thing."

The men's faces were turning color.

"Rats. Yes, rats are fitting, though they aren't very artistic, are they? Shame. Oh well, I hope you enjoy what's left of your new life."

She raised the two up into the air, clenching her grip around Marcus' throat tighter and tighter. "No one will see your paintings, and no one will idolize your talent. You will see people run from you, terrified that my little Black Death will show itself again."

Selena dropped the two oafs. She didn't feel like hearing them beg, so she snapped her fingers on both hands and poof, two pathetic rats scurried out the door.

Selena slowly walked up the stairs and entered the loft to find her daughter dead for the second time.

"I am sorry, Vanessa. I thought Marcus would be part of a safe environment for you to grow up in. Well, we shouldn't dwell in the past. Shall we start anew?" Selena blew her a kiss just like before, but this time, she vanished with Vanessa.

Salem Witch Trials

"Come inside. Get out of the rain." A weathered-looking woman welcomed her guest into her quaint home in the woods. "What do we have here?" The guest was carrying what looked like her laundry, but it was moving.

"I heard crying on my way to see you, so I wanted to check it out. Wouldn't you know…" the guest unraveled the bundle of rags and linens, "it was a baby girl making all that racket."

"Oh, my."

"Helen, I can't keep her. I mean, could you imagine my husband? We already have 5 kids…"

"Don't you worry, hun. I can take care of her." Helen reached out her arms as her guest placed the now much happier baby in her arms. The baby looked up at Helen. There was something about the baby's eyes…a twinkle of magic maybe…that calmed Helen. The baby smiled at her. "Hello, little Vanessa."

The baby cooed.

"Oh, you like that name, don't you? And you have such a unique necklace. Yes, you do. You are special, aren't you? Now what can I get for you, Margaret?"

"One of the kids has a fever."

"Alright, hun." Helen walked over to her shelves while bouncing the baby in her arm at the same time to keep the baby calm. "Here is a mixture of peppermint, ginger, and some cinnamon. Make a tea with it and give it to him right away. It'll help him sweat it out. Tomorrow morning, rub this on his chest." Helen handed Margaret a paste in a small jar. "It has eucalyptus, spearmint, and chamomile."

"Thank you Helen. After everything you've done for our family, we can't thank you enough."

"Of course, no need to fret. He'll be just fine."

The two women hugged. Margaret said goodbye to the little girl, then headed back home to her own brood.

Once Helen saw Margaret had vanished into the foggy woods, she turned her focus onto Vanessa.

"Oh, my child, you are a special one. I can tell; you and I are very much alike. Let's put some clothes on you. I had a feeling I would need some baby clothes. Now I see the premonition was for you." Helen picked up a dress and took off Vanessa's ragged clothes. Helen lay the child down, and the baby's back chilled from the wooden table.

Gasp

"You poor child. You have seen much horror in your lives, haven't you?" Helen looked at Vanessa's leg and noticed the jagged shreddings. There was a faint pin-dot red mark on her chest. "I wonder what this is…"

Helen lifted Vanessa up onto her shoulder, like holding a sack of potatoes, in order to button up the back of the dress.

"Oh, Vanessa." Helen placed her trembling hand onto a bulbous, morphed clump of skin on Vanessa's back. "You suffered much from hands who were meant to keep you safe. This must be the beginning of the scar that leads through your heart to your chest. You couldn't have deserved such betrayal."

Helen cradled the baby's soft head, comforting what must have been a horrible ending to Vanessa's last life. "That life was recent, wasn't it? The scar looks bothered, warm and red. I promise I will care for you."

Helen finished buttoning up the dress.

"You must be hungry. Who knows how long you were out there all by yourself?" Helen mixed some cow's milk and water. Vanessa fussed and pushed it away.

"I know, my dear, but you must eat."

Vanessa pushed away again.

"Oh dear, I must look into getting a wet nurse then. I shouldn't think it'll be difficult. I help many mamas and Lord knows, they keep having those babies. Perhaps I should just ask Margaret. She found you to begin with. She doesn't know it yet, but she is with child. I can give her some fenugreek to speed up the feeding production…Yes, I think I'll visit with her tomorrow and inform her of the good news."

"Good morning, Maragret. How are you feeling this morning?"

"Not sure, to be honest. Last night I started cramping. I've never had that much pain while pregnant. You telling me I was pregnant 4 months ago wasn't the best of news, but I warmed up to another little one roaming around the house. Now, I'm concerned this one may not make it." Margaret stumbled. Thankfully, Helen grabbed her arm to stabilize her.

"Sit down, hun. Let me take a look at you."

"I'll sit, but hand me Vanessa. Let's get her fed first."

Once Vanessa was fed, Helen placed her hands on Margaret's stomach. She then leaned down to listen to the baby dwelling inside.

"I'm so sorry, Margaret. I don't feel any movement."

Vanessa cried.

"Wait, look."

Margaret's belly shifted. Helen listened again, placing her ear on Margaret's stomach.

Thump

Helen sighed in relief and let out a short laugh as the baby kicked Helen's head. "I think the baby has found a friend. It seems the baby likes to talk to little Vanessa."

"What is the cramping from then?"

"You have been pregnant many times, but none have been back to back. You are feeding while you are with child. Some cramping can be normal, hun. This is a novel experience for you. I have a feeling you'll be just fine."

"Thank you, Helen. It is nice to have such a good friend. I am glad that your little Vanessa has found a friend already." As Margaret held Vanessa in her arms, Helen could sense the beginnings of a long history forming between them. Though she couldn't see into the future, there was something about Vanessa that made Helen think she had already lived a long life and there was more to come.

"Have you thought of a name?"

"If it is a boy, Henry. If it is a girl…Mildred."

"Mildred, it will be then."

"Oh my, you can tell."

"Yes, and these two will be the best of friends."

"Helen?" Vanessa creeped from behind her room curtain.

"Yes, Vanessa."

"Why don't I call you mom?"

"That's an odd question, but it has a simple answer. I'm not your mother."

"I've never had a mom, you know, in any of my lives."

"No?"

Vanessa shook her head. "My papa raised me in my first life, and a drunk in my next…never a mother. The only constant in my life has been this necklace…and my name." Vanessa fidgeted with her butterfly necklace as she revealed her humble, yet unusual past.

"I'm sure, when the time is right, you'll find your answers."

A sparrow flew in through the always open doorway and landed on Helen's shoulders. Helen turned to welcome the sparrow. Helen winked at the bird and smiled, but then noticed the disappointment on Vanessa's sweet face.

"Come here. Come sit with me."

Vanessa walked with her head down, shuffling her feet as she walked toward Helen, then she sat on Helen's lap as she was told.

"You are a powerful witch, yet full of a kindness that is so untouched by the evils of the world. I am sure your mother, wherever she is, loves you very much. In the meantime…," Helen checked in with the sparrow, as if asking for permission.

The sparrow chirped.

"how about you call me Mama Helen?"

A brightness came back to Vanessa's face.

"Now, what shall we do today?"

"Well…let me think. I remember lots of what Papa taught me. So, I'm not sure. What can you teach me?"

"Hmm…your dad taught you about using nature's energy, yes? Have you ever used your own?"

"No, Papa said it would take a toll on my body."

"Mmmm, that it might…which is why you must learn your limits. Let's go outside, I'll show you."

Vanessa slid off of Mama Helen's lap, then ran outside. Mama Helen cringed as she stood from her chair. With her first step, she winced as a jolt shot up from her heels to hip, up the spine, and to the base of her neck. The pain subsided the more she walked. The sparrow took flight once Mama Helen got closer to the door, then it landed on a nearby branch to witness the magic show.

Vanessa couldn't stand still while she waited for Mama Helen to appear in the shady cove of their front yard. "I'm ready, Mama Helen. I know I can do this."

"I know you can, my child. But first, you must listen."

Vanessa stopped dancing about and attempted to stand still to listen to her instructions.

"Your mind, body, and heart are all powerful on their own, but when you connect them into a singular unit, anything is possible."

Vanessa started bouncing around again.

"Calm yourself, Vanessa. You'll need that bubbly energy."

Vanessa stopped once again.

"Close your eyes. Be at peace in your mind and heart."

The eager girl did as she was told.

"Think about floating an object of your choice…keeping yourself calm. Once you think of the object you want, lift your hands as though you are holding an enormous ball."

Vanessa raised her arms to shoulder height, and spread her fingers as if trying to grasp the moon.

"Vanessa, keep your concentration, but open your eyes."

Hundreds of flowers, of every color and species, hovered right in front of them.

"Mama Helen, look, look. I'm doing it."

As Vanessa's excitement grew, the flowers sank back to the earth. "What happened?"

"You did a grand job." It surprised Helen that she had unearthed a field. A novice witch would not only fail to lift the object off the ground on the first attempt, but it would be a singular object at best. "You let your emotions cloud your concentration. Over time, and with much practice, you'll be able to focus and keep yourself balanced."

"So, why did Papa think it was dangerous?"

"Using your energy can be dangerous, but only if you practice your magic with just one part of yourself like only your heart, or only your mind. Synchronizing all three gives you a bigger energy pool to pull from, thereby taking longer for you to grow lethargic." Helen breathed with struggle. "How about you go play with Millie? Mama Helen needs to lie down."

"Okay." Vanessa bounced to Mama Helen and kissed her on the cheek. Then she skipped to town to play with her friend.

"Vanessa! Over here," a nearby shout rang out through the woods. Vanessa stopped skipping and looked around.

Sparrow was flapping next to her.

"Vanessa." A girl waved both arms in the air, then started running towards Vanessa.

"Millie, I was just coming to see you."

"Me too." The girls giggled as they hugged.

"You want to see something fantastic?"

"Oh, yes."

Vanessa closed her eyes and remembered what she had learned earlier. "Calm and unite, calm and unite," Vanessa repeated in her head.

"Vanessa, how are you doing that?"

"Pretty amazing, isn't it?" Vanessa opened her eyes and saw a boulder levitating in front of them. Vanessa slowly lowered her hands. They watched as the boulder followed her lead, like a stringed puppet, then settled back onto the ground.

"Want to play now?"

"Yes, let's go to the creek."

The two girls held hands, then dashed off for a swim in the creek about a mile away. Their feathered friend shadowed them.

"Water is so much harder to control when it's not a cohesive unit." Vanessa had been practicing using her own energy for years now, but water seemed to have a mind of its own.

Chirp

"I have used water before in my first life, but it was as a unit. I made one solid shield and even then, I drew from it using its energy, not mine. Dancing droplets are proving to be more difficult."

Chip, Chirp

"Quiet, Sparrow, let me try again."

Vanessa slowed her breathing. Closed her eyes. "Calm and unite."

This time, she lowered her body, almost touching the water with her palms. As she rose and rippled her fingers ever so softly, she could feel the spray of the water hitting her face. Vanessa opened her eyes. Water droplets were dancing in unison with the pumping of her fingertips.

Chirp, Chirp, Chirp

The sparrow joined the water show; it darted amongst the suspended water.

"I finally did it."

Vanessa played with the water until the sun and water combo stopped dancing around her with their radiating prism colors.

"Time to head home, Sparrow."

Vanessa dropped the water all at once, making it splash the sparrow and herself.

"Oops," Vanessa laughed as she rang out her hair. Sparrow landed on Vanessa's head and shook its feathers.

Vanessa hummed all the way back home with Sparrow chiming in, of course.

When they got closer to their hut, Vanessa saw a hand on the ground sticking out over the threshold.

"Mama Helen." Vanessa ran over to find that Helen had fallen. Her breathing was weak and inconsistent, but her eyes never left Vanessa's. She picked up Mama Helen's head and rested it on her knees.

"You…are strong…and kind," Helen's voice crackled. "Use your beautiful gifts…to continue our work. I love you…my daughter." Her last breath escaped her tired body. Vanessa clung to her; the closest thing she had ever had to a mother.

Tears soaked Mama Helen's forehead as Vanessa graced her with a tender kiss. "I love you too. I won't let you down."

"Millie, can you see who is outside?"

"I don't hear anything…"

"Trust me, someone is out there. They need help. I'll be right there. I just need to finish up with Mrs. Smith."

"If you say so…"

Millie went outside. She spotted a woman on the ground, groaning in pain.

"Vanessa," Millie yelled, "she needs help now."

Vanessa was by the woman's side in an instant. "Let me look at you, hun. What troubles you?"

The woman's leg looked out of place, but Vanessa noticed the woman holding her shoulder as well. Bruises covered her ribs and throat, as if someone had strangled her after severely beating her body with something like a fire iron or some other heavy object. She couldn't imagine anyone purposely hurting another living soul. Who could possibly be that cruel?

"Poor dear," Millie crooned. "Should we get her inside?"

"No, that could cause more damage and just add more unnecessary pain. I will help her here. Millie, go give Mrs. Smith the lavender and chamomile to help her get some much needed rest, then quickly return. I'll need your help keeping this one calm."

When Millie left, Vanessa brushed the hair off of the visitor's worn-out face. "You have traveled far for help, my dear. I am sorry for your hardship, and for what I must do to help you. But I promise I will heal you."

Millie ran back out. The two friends waited for Mrs. Smith to be out of sight before they started assisting the broken woman.

"Millie, you must hold her still so that I can mend the bone properly. Any movement may cause it to heal crooked. Do not let go of her, understand?"

"Yes," Millie replied.

The woman screamed when Millie took hold of her leg.

"I am sorry." Millie squinted her eyes as she couldn't imagine that pain the woman was in.

Vanessa took a breath in. She slowed her own anxious heart to a speed equivalent to pouring honey, then she gently placed her hand on the battered leg.

Millie witnessed the shift in her leg as the bone snapped back into place. The visitor screamed, her cries bouncing off of the trees, but Millie held her steady. Vanessa started at the woman's hip, compressing the leg between her hands, all the way down to her ankle. The leg twitched as it responded to the healing. Vanessa then moved her position to get a better look at the woman's shoulder. It had popped out of socket.

"I need you to sit up so I can care for your shoulder."

Millie assisted the woman to a sitting position. Vanessa went behind her and squeezed her shoulder. The shoulder snapped back into place. After hearing and feeling the grinding of bones, the woman yelled out again, then soon passed out.

"Is she alright?"

"Her body is weak, she needs rest…as do I. Mending bones apparently takes more power than dancing water. No more visitors today, Millie; I won't be much help to them in this state. You can head back home to your mom. Tell her I say, 'hello'."

"I will, Vanessa. You are a wonderful person."

Vanessa smiled at her friend. Her eyes were heavy, and her skin wasn't as bright as it usually was.

The two of them picked up the woman and laid her inside on the bed. Once Millie left, Vanessa laid next to the bed on the ground, gratefully shut her eyes, and closed off her mind.

"Mom, you'll never guess what Vanessa did today."

"Oh?"

"She fixed a broken leg."

Margaret turned around. "She did what? How could that be possible?"

"I don't know how she does it, but she is great at helping people."

"That is against God. Only witches can do that…only those who have sold themselves to the devil."

"No…she's not like that. You know her. She's like a daughter."

"I don't want you around her anymore. I forbid it."

"You fed her like you fed me. Please don't do this. She is my friend."

"I forbid it." Margaret looked at her daughter as if she was reciting a commandment from God. Her face was ridged and lacked an ounce of loss for someone whom she once cared for deeply.

Millie burst into tears and ran to her room. She heard a knock on the house's door.

"Oh, hello…" Margaret wasn't expecting anyone. She fanned herself with her hand, still shocked by the news that Millie had just shared.

"Are you alright?" the visitor asked.

"No, I have just received some unsettling news. My daughter told me…just now…" Margaret fumbled, trying to find a chair to sit upon before she passed out.

Millie did her best to listen through the walls. *Sounds like the schoolteacher*, Millie thought. *What's she doing here?*

"Margaret, how can I help?" The teacher navigated Margaret to a chair.

"I believe there is a witch in our town. I can't believe this person would do such an evil act, but my daughter is no liar."

"Who is it, Margaret? We must tell the preacher."

The two women sat while Margaret had a battle between her heart and her mind. "I'll tell the preacher myself. Come with me."

Millie heard the door shut, then lock behind them. "Let me out, mother!" She left her room to bang on the door.

"I can't risk you warning her. Vanessa must be punished for her sins. I refuse to let you get tangled in her dark web." The women left Millie in thoughts of guilt.

Millie tried to break out of her house, but nothing worked. She sat up against the door. *What have I done? This is all my fault. How could I have done this to my best friend?* She repeated her guilt-ridden mantra over and over as she rocked back and forth while hugging her knees. She wondered how one innocent statement could turn into something so dangerous and so wicked when all she wanted to do was share how proud she was of her dear friend, the healer. After some time, Millie heard a tapping at the door.

Chirp

"Sparrow?"

Chirp, Chirp

She heard the door unlock.

"You are a smart bird, aren't you? Now come quickly, we must warn Vanessa."

Millie ran as fast as she could while Sparrow almost struggled to keep up.

"Vanessa, Vanessa." Millie shouted as quietly as possible.

Vanessa appeared in the doorway. The sparrow started pulling at her dress immediately.

"Calm yourselves. What is going on?"

The sun peeked over the horizon and fog clouded the surrounding forest.

"I'm so sorry, Vanessa. I didn't know."

"Millie, what are you talking about?"

"I told my mom about the miracle you performed today, and now she thinks you're a witch. She and the teacher left to inform the preacher, but that was a while ago. You must leave this place, Vanessa. I pray you can find it in your heart to forgive my naivete and thoughtlessness. I never wanted to hurt you."

Vanessa hugged her friend. Floating fire light advanced on the friend—it was too late.

Before they knew it, they were being pulled apart; Margaret was pulling her daughter while two townsmen restrained Vanessa. The mood quieted as the preacher stepped forward.

He faced Vanessa. She could feel his blinded fear and hatred piercing her soul.

"Are you a witch?"

Vanessa didn't know what to do. She had never lied before. It went against her moral compass, but could she risk whatever consequence she would have to endure? *Granted, I'd probably just come back and live a new life if the worst result is death,* she thought. A smirk appeared on her face, not realizing that she had shown outward emotions to her thoughts.

"Do you think this is funny?" he asked with a firm slap across her face.

Vanessa gritted her teeth. She could feel the tingling warmth rising to her cheek. "No sir," she forced.

"Then answer my question."

Vanessa looked at Millie and Margaret. Millie's face was soaked in tears. Margaret couldn't even look back at Vanessa. Margaret's eyes were sad, but her body was trembling at the same time.

Vanessa remembered the women whom she had helped just hours prior. How did this day come to such a conclusion? Would this mob punish the innocent woman as well? Was I supposed to let her die a horrible death?

The preacher raised his hand again and slapped the same cheek. "If you won't answer, we'll have to find out the truth for ourselves." He turned, then nodded his head to the crowd. A few of the townspeople threw their torches into her house.

"No," Vanessa cried. The last time she checked, the woman she was caring for was still sleeping on the bed in her cottage. Vanessa thrashed about, trying to free herself from the grasp of the men who held her. Each time she got a chance, she flung herself towards the burning house, only to be caught again. Finally, in one of her attempts, she saw the woman fleeing out of what would have been Vanessa's small window. The woman ran with no limp…her healing was complete.

Somehow, that made Vanessa feel relieved. She didn't much care about her fate at this point. She prayed that the woman would escape, allowing her to create a new life for herself. Vanessa stopped struggling to free herself and waited until her captors grabbed hold of her once more and secured her bindings.

As they walked along the path away from the house, the pink hues of the sunrise softened the menacing flames she had left behind. Eventually, they all came to a halt when they happened upon a lake. As Venessa looked around her surroundings, she realized the creek where she and Millie played as children flowed into this very lake not far away.

Vanessa finally heard Sparrow. She assumed the bird was with them the whole time, but the sunrise had preoccupied her mind. *Odd how the bird always seems to know what is going on*, Vanessa daydreamed. *How is it that this bird, the same kind, has befriended me in each life thus far?*

Reality soon made itself known by someone jerking her tied hands and leading her to the edge of the lake. The coarse rope dug into her skin.

"Tie her feet as well, then tie the other end of the rope around this boulder. If she can get out of this and swim up to the surface, then we'll know that she is indeed a witch. If she drowns…well…we'll know she wasn't," he motioned. *An odd kind of syllogism,* she mused. *With that logic, I'm either a witch and they'll kill me anyway, or I'll already be dead. Brilliant.*

Vanessa didn't fight them. Millie thought her friend was oddly calm.

Four men waded out into the water until they were at waist height, then they tossed her and the boulder into the deepest part of the water. Vanessa's hair unraveled from her bun with the current of the water. She could see the preacher's face fade as she sank lower.

Calm and unite, calm and unite.

When the preacher's face was no longer in sight, she released herself from her confines and swam, holding her breath for as long as she could… *Calm and unite.*

"Air," her lungs yelled. She couldn't hold it any longer. She finally breached the surface, breathing in the oxygen she so desperately needed; the air was harsh, as if her lungs weren't able to expand quickly enough to take it in, but she knew she had to be careful of making too much noise. She was aware she was out of the town, but she wanted to make sure no one else was around her. Once clear, she headed for the water's edge.

Chirp, Chirp

"You have piqued my interest, Sparrow. I'm getting the feeling that you and I go way back…I mean…way back. But if that is the case, then you'd have to be magical as well. Who are you?"

It was as if the sun shone brighter than it ever had, focusing its light on the bird. Gold dust swirled around the ball of energy shooting sparks of light this way and that. Once it finally dulled, Vanessa squinted as she opened her eyes.

"You're…a fairy?"

"Oh, but I'm so much more. My name is Selena. It is true, a beautiful fairy I am, but I am also a queen. And if that's not enough…I'm also your mother."

Vanessa just stood there—knee deep in the water as she absentmindedly twisted her hair to wring out the water.

"Come sit with me? I'm sure you have questions…and I have the answers."

Vanessa still didn't move.

"Or…I can come to you. How about I just start from the beginning? Your father and I loved each other very much, no matter if the time was short or semi-arranged…" Selena's words trailed off as her mind wandered.

"Arranged?"

Selena straightened up. Now wasn't the time to go into details. "Nevermind that. The point is, he is the reason I wanted to have a family. He showed me the power of love."

"Sure didn't take you long to leave…" Vanessa finally blurted as she took giant-sized steps toward shore, leaving her mom in the water.

"You didn't inherit my bloodline like I hoped…like I thought you would. I still had a kingdom to run."

"So…what…you were just going to take me if I had your blood and abandon dad? Glad I didn't make the cut."

"I understand your hostility—really I do, but what was I supposed to do? I couldn't leave my subjects. They needed me to help them rebuild everything we had lost."

"Yeah, I turned out great, apparently. I've only died twice already and barely escaped a third. Perfect life right here, folks." Vanessa bowed repeatedly, changing directions to appease the nonexistent audience.

"I have been with you. I know a bird may not be the best way to show my support, but I have tried to be there for you. It broke my heart seeing that man kill you. As for the dragon,"

"You shouldn't have distracted me by torturing Tristan."

"True. I apologize for that. I was jealous…"

The conversation took a pause as Vanessa took some time just remembering everything she had gone through.

"You were there a lot…my first friend. We talked about everything. I saw you try to warn me about the butcher. I just wasn't quick enough."

Selena smiled. "I'm glad you thought of us as friends."

"I have a question."

"Of course…anything."

"I can see that you like the color purple, given your…attire, so I assume this necklace has something to do with you?"

"My gift to you before I left." Selena floated closer to Vanessa and held the necklace in her glittered hand. "I wanted to spend as much time with you as I would have if you had ended up with my bloodline. I enchanted this pendant so that you would reincarnate when you died. It protects you from the deaths of this world. I was expecting you to live much longer in each life, but you are strong-willed and quite the adventurer, so dragons and a fame-deprived artist weren't what I was expecting. This…," Selena still held the butterfly pendant, "follows you into each lifetime. It is a part of you. You cannot be separated."

"Why didn't you reveal yourself earlier?"

"I promised your father that I wouldn't until I felt like you really needed or wanted me. I had to leave your side often enough, so I agreed. You needed someone more stable to care for you in your younger years. I knew I couldn't provide that, so I kept my identity a secret, as promised. But now, well, you pretty much just asked the bird…well…me who I was, and so here I am."

"Fair enough."

"Do you have any more questions?"

Vanessa thought for a moment. She had one, but wasn't sure she wanted to know the answer. She politely took the pendant out of her mother's hand and paced, keeping parallel to the shoreline.

"Yes, one more."

Selena nodded, then waited for Vanessa to proceed.

"What did you sacrifice for such an enchantment to give me the opportunity of multiple lives?"

"I sacrificed nothing. I'm still me, a queen. I still have my subjects and my kingdom, and with this necklace, I still have you."

"So who, or what is being sacrificed when I come back in another life?"

Selena cocked her head a little with a raised eyebrow. "What are you talking about?"

"Where one thing is created, another must be sacrificed. This is to keep the balance in every living thing in the world. Lucian…Papa… taught me that. So I'm asking, when I return in another life, what is being sacrificed to maintain the balance of the world?"

Selena, after being able to learn about her daughter over a few lifetimes, knew that Vanessa would not be pleased with the answer. "I hope you understand. This was my way of being a part of your life. You'd be surprised at how durable these humans can be."

"What is it?" Vanessa drilled her mother, not letting her leave the question unanswered.

"I don't want to lie to you."

"So don't."

"You won't like it."

Vanessa faced her, arms crossed in front of her chest. She tapped her foot and pursed her lips together.

"Kindness. The world's kindness, to be precise."

"I can't believe you."

"Well, I am the Queen of the Dark Fairies…the sacrifices weren't a priority of mine, nor were they going to be good."

"Wait, you are a dark fairy queen?"

"Did I not mention the 'dark' part before?"

"So let me get this straight…You, the Queen of the Dark Fairies, married Lucian, my father, who was a good warlock. You then abandoned me when I wasn't up to your standards, but to make you feel better about ditching us, you 'gifted' me with a curse that drains the goodness and happiness out of the world in which I live…repeatedly…thereby causing hate and war and leaving the world darker and more damaged in each life than it was before? Does that about sum it up?"

Vanessa didn't let her mother answer. "Or was this your plan all along? Am I just your tool to cause the darkness, so that you can be the supreme ruler of the world and wipe out humanity."

"I tried that already, but your father got in the way of those plans too."

Vanessa let her jaw drop. Unsure if she wanted to scream at her mother or vomit at the utter disregard for life. "You should have kept your promise to Papa longer. I want nothing to do with you." Vanessa closed her eyes. "Calm and unite."

"Vanessa, don't do this."

"Calm and unite, calm and unite," Vanessa recited her verse louder and louder. In the very second that Vanessa had closed off her mind to her wicked mother, she disappeared.

Selena could no longer see her daughter.

Vanessa didn't move…she didn't even breathe. She watched as the queen morphed herself into a bird again and flew away.

Loneliness. This is what it was like. Not only was she now invisible to her mother, but she was now also invisible to the world. Friends were no longer possible for fear Selena would find her and give her mother the satisfaction of seeing her. Before leaving the area entirely, Vanessa wanted to say goodbye to Millie. Vanessa didn't want her friend to feel bad for telling Margaret about her special abilities.

Vanessa ran back into town. She peered into Millie's window. Millie was sitting at the edge of her bed, staring into nothingness, as if in a trance. Her eyes were red and swollen, but her tears still stained her face. Vanessa tapped on the window to get Millie's attention. Once Millie was looking in her direction, she picked up a rock and held it in front of her. Millie's curiosity at the floating rock turned to realization and she ran to the window.

"Vanessa," Millie whispered.

As the rock slowly came towards Millie, she reached out her hand, and Vanessa placed the rock in Millie's palm.

"Be well, Vanessa." Millie breathed out. Her shoulders relaxed, and a smile appeared. It warmed Vanessa's heart.

Vanessa spun around and around, causing a small whirlwind. Both girls giggled, remembering their childhood shenanigans.

The dust settled, and Millie waved farewell.

Vanessa wandered the lands, watching the life that she could no longer participate in pass her by. Finding a home was easy, as she didn't need much. She finally came to a stone bridge that allowed a small creek to gently flow beneath it. It was as close to a home as she could manage given her current invisibility.

A year passed by, and Vanessa wasn't certain if she could be alone much longer. But what other choice did she have? Though she had made some new friends—those of the fur and feathered sort—she now knew to stay away from sparrows. With the animals, the conversations lacked…content and satisfaction…well, the give and take aspect of the conversations at least. Bunnies just sat in her lap, waiting to be petted. The squirrels would visit just to get some food. A blue jay popped in from time to time, but it mainly just watched from afar.

Vanessa had made her new home comfortable; she even took up a hobby: gardening. She wanted to get back to her roots, so to speak. Lavender, heather, and honeysuckle were her favorites. The flowers calmed her, but they also aided in the strength of the protection spell.

"Why, hello there. Finally decided to join the party?"

The blue jay went right up to her and landed in the dirt that Vanessa was tilling. The bird started to glow. Brighter and brighter.

"Not again…" Vanessa protested as she stood, and backed away from the bird, giving whatever or whomever she was going to meet some space.

Dark blue glitter swirled around the glow, just like Selena. Finally, the firework show stopped.

"A dark fairy, I presume?"

"Aren't you the clever one?"

"You all sure know how to make an entrance…no doubt about that."

"Thank you." The fairy curtsied. Her outfit was a bit more revealing than Selena's—a deep blue three-quarter sleeve top with a black leather corset around her tiny waist, and a tutu, of all things. It, too, sparkled her blue hue with a black ribbon trimming its hem. Her wings looked similar to Selena's, so the fundamental difference was the color scheme.

"Not a fan of purple?" Vanessa spat as she turned to continue her gardening.

"No, that's more mom's preference."

Vanessa dropped her tools and wondered if she had heard that correctly. "What was that you just said?"

The fairy repositioned herself to face Vanessa. As she fluttered over, her bouncy ringlets seemed to defy gravity.

"I'm Lillian, your twin sister."

Vanessa felt all the blood rush out of her head. There was no way to be 'calm and united' at this point in time.

"How…" Vanessa couldn't even finish one line of thought. So many questions buzzed in and out of her head.

"Let me sum up all of your questions for you, sis. Wouldn't want you to pass out or anything. Before mom had you, the night we were born, she had me. Lucian was fetching water and I popped out. Mother stopped time, giving her a chance to pass me to a fairy midwife of sorts since she knew I was of the obviously more superior bloodline. She had hoped you would be the same. While she knew she was pregnant with twins, Father didn't. He had only heard one heartbeat after all. Which concerned Mother, but there was still a chance. But as the time spell faded, Lucian entered the home and you popped out as human. You can imagine Mother's disappointment.

Vanessa's blood was now rushing to her head quite quickly. The cruel comments from her sister were turning her face red.

"Mom left you for her kingdom, like she told you, but also for me. I was her only hope at that point to take over the kingdom when the time came. To be honest, I'm not sure what she sees in you. I've observed you for some time now, and I have to say…you live quite a boring life."

"I wouldn't have such a boring life if I didn't have to hide from our mother."

"Why are you being so ungrateful? She loves you, for reasons unclear to me, so what if she gave you a gift that takes rainbows and daisies out of the world…why should you care? They are just humans."

"Part of being a witch is being a human. I have a heart just like them."

"I have a heart too."

"Are you sure about that?" Vanessa took her chance to be snarky.

"Aww, you think you're funny too, how human-like." Lillian rolled her eyes. "My point is, unlike humans, you have a gift to be immortal. Well, in a way. Plus, you have power. So why stoop to their level and try to help them?"

"It's in my nature. Guess there really is no doubt about whose bloodline we each have. Wait…"

"I can see the wheels turning in that witchy brain of yours. I even know what you're going to ask, but I really want to hear the words come out of your mouth." The corners of Lillian's mouth curled. Vanessa swore she could see dancing blue flames where a heart should be. Lillian crouched down, leaning ever so slightly on one of her hands while the other rested on her knee. She waited like a hawk ready to pounce on its prey.

"How did you find me?"

"We have a winner, folks." Lillian applauded.

"I have protection, not even mom can see me."

"It all comes down to blood. We may not share the same powers…" Lillian looked up and down Vanessa, "or fashion sense, but we have 100% the same blood. Twins…remember? It acts like….what's that thing when you people use sticks to find water?"

"Dowsing?"

"Yes, dowsing. I move in a direction, and a glitter trail just lights up for me."

"Great. Dare I ask why you have decided to grace me with your presence?"

"Well…"

"Actually, why did you wait so long?"

"That's a much easier question to answer. Mom thought you needed some time alone."

"O…kay. You can answer the other question now."

"That one is a bit more sticky. You see, Mom misses you." Lillian started circling Vanessa, lightly touching her shoulders and back. "She thinks you've had enough time in timeout, and is hoping that you will stop hiding."

"One year. She thinks one year of 'timeout', as you put it, is all it takes to get over her highness' selfishness? It's going to take a few more lifetimes for that to be at the back of my mind, sister."

Lillian was behind Vanessa now, caressing her hair.

"The answer is a firm, 'no'."

"See, I was hoping you'd make this easy for me, but now I have to get bloody."

Lillian grabbed Vanessa's hair and hiked her up to a levitated fairy height. Vanessa gasped at the yank. She could feel the hairs at the base of her neck being plucked one by one like the strings of a guitar popping when tuned too tight. Lillian took her finger and raised it in front of Vanessa. Lillian's nail grew right in front of Vanessa's eyes.

The tip shaped into a point; rhinestones multiplying to cover the extended dagger.

"What are you doing, Lillian?"

"I told you. Mom wants to see you. This is the only way for that to happen, since you don't want to come out from behind your security blanket."

"You're going to kill me?"

"Yes, but hey…I'll see you next time." With no more talk left to do, Lillian sliced her sister's throat. Vanessa gargled for a couple of seconds while her blood spray splattered her flowers. Lillian dropped her sister's shell, then licked the blood off her nail.

"Such a foul thing, human blood."

Roaring 20's

"My poor child. Let's bring you inside the house and clean you up."

The headmistress brought the baby girl into the crowded house, then headed for the sink. Other children were crying, yelling, and running around. "Don't you worry about them. That rowdy bunch will soon head off to bed. We have a big day tomorrow, you know. You came at just the right time." The headmistress ran some water, then removed the baby's swaddlings.

"Oh, dear." The headmistress noticed the scarring around the baby's leg, on her back and chest, and… The headmistress picked up the butterfly necklace, and held it in her hand. "How curious you are. But…oh…what is this?" She lifted the necklace, just enough to see a long, thin scar in the shape of a smile that ran across the child's neck. "How could someone do something so horrid to such a precious child?"

The baby cried as the headmistress lightly brushed the raised ridge with her fingertip.

"Oh, it's okay, little one. I've got you now. Whoever did this to you will get their just rewards soon enough. God knows their sin, don't you worry. Unfortunately, given your disfigurement, I doubt anyone will want to foster you. I think I should raise you as my own. What do you think of that?"

The baby had calmed down. Headmistress continued to wash the baby up. "I'll teach you all the good we are going to do with this 'Orphan Train'. Now, since you will be my responsibility, you may call me Miss Hughes instead of Headmistress. And what shall we call you? Hmm…how about Vanessa, what do you think?"

The baby yawned as Miss Hughes wrapped her up in a clean blanket and rocked Vanessa to sleep.

"Miss Hughes, I am 15 years old now. You know I can be on my own," Vanessa pleaded.

After all, I have been on my own for several lifetimes now; I know how to take care of myself. Have you not noticed that you barely had to raise me, and I have successfully taken part in assisting in placing these kids? She thought all this in her head, of course. There is no way she'd get away with talking like that to Miss Hughes. She was kind and tender, but she had strict rules about backtalk, cleanliness, and chores.

She remembered more things quicker this time around than any other life. It was as if Vanessa had picked up right where she left off with the last life, minus the treacherous dark fairy family, of course. She would see the nasty birds from time to time, but thankfully, the train moved quicker than their bird forms could handle. Vanessa had no desire to affiliate with them. She simply ignored their chirping.

"Vanessa, we have talked about this since you have been able to speak, which was quite young. Nevertheless, the answer is still the same. No. I took you in as my own child, so until you are at least 18 years of age, I dare say you're stuck with me. And these helpless children need you. You have been great in helping me care and coordinate homes for them. They, we, would feel lost without you."

"Ahhh."

"Excuse me, young lady?"

"Sorry. Yes, ma'am." Vanessa marched off to the back of the train. It was her favorite place, in this lifetime at any rate. The fast-paced change in scenery reminded her of her paintings. The wind blowing through her hair gave her a sense of freedom even though she resided in narrow iron walls on wheels. She picked up her necklace and rubbed one of the butterfly's wings with her fingers. Feeling the bumps of the green stones was a constant reminder of the gift she was cursed with. However, Vanessa did see some good…this time, anyway. The "Orphan Train" had placed many children in suitable homes so far. Vanessa felt good being a part of it even though she knew that somewhere else in the world, people were suffering because of her new life in this era. It was, after all, an imbalance.

Chirp

"I honestly can't believe you would think that it is alright for you to be following me after everything you have done."

The sparrow made itself comfy on the guardrail of the caboose.

"Look, if I'm going to be alive for a while, which last I checked I have eternity, can't you give me a good 100 years or so? Then maybe we can revisit your persistent mission of making my life miserable."

Chirp

"I guess if you won't leave, I'll have to." Vanessa turned on her heels and went back inside her mobile jail. She sat in a vacant seat and daydreamed as she looked at the morning landscape, still fidgeting with her cursed necklace.

"Vanessa," Miss Hughes called. "We need your help in here."

"So much for dreaming. Probably a poopy diaper I need to change."

Drawn out cries of the train's whistle blew out, alerting the sleeping Vanessa that they were entering New York City. She loved being in the city. Sure, she had been in one in Italy during the Renaissance, but it couldn't compare to the buildings that appeared to touch the clouds. The hustle and bustle was even different. Everything was a rush, business -like, and drained of social interaction. And though she had been in New York City quite a few times in this life, it never stopped her from feeling like a kid in a candy shop. After all, the city was forever changing. There was always something new to see.

Maybe the city would prove to be better suited for my lifestyle. Birds don't like the city, right? she pondered. There were still a handful of orphans they weren't able to place, but they would just rejoin the new flock of kids the following day when they headed out west again.

"Vanessa, I need you."

"I know, I'll get provisions: diapers, bread, a couple of clothes big enough to fit all, and some fruit if I have any money left. Anything else?"

"No, that covers it. Thanks, Vanessa."

"That's what I'm here for…" Vanessa grabbed a bag and the money from Miss Hughes' purse, then headed down the train's metal steps.

The busyness on the street reminded Vanessa of bugs in the forest, only the bugs seemed to care more about their surroundings. People in the big city seemed to just purposely and carelessly bump into each other, or they just passed each other by, not knowing or caring what secrets others had hidden in their lives.

At the same time, it was an appreciable change of pace.

So much time has passed since my last life. Vanessa wondered if it was a sort of punishment from her mom.

Chirp

Vanessa heard from a distance. She looked all around her, but saw nothing.

Chirp it sang again.

Vanessa looked up. The sparrow was hovering over her rather than beside her.

"Do you really think I suffered from a pause in my eternal life? I couldn't care less at this point. If anything, you just prolonged seeing me, and wasn't that the entire purpose of our lovely family reunion with my twin sister? Just leave me alone." Vanessa picked up her pace, darting between the blindly walking humans on her way to the store.

After gathering items for Miss Hughes, Vanessa figured she'd enjoy some time alone. She sat on a park bench and dreamed of what might be her future home as she observed the people walking through the park. The dresses the women wore were short compared to what she was used to——so revealing in the chest and arm areas…and those legs… There was so much bare skin shown. The women adorned themselves with beads and jewels in their hair and on their bodies, and their faces were enhanced with some kind of paint. They were beautiful though, like porcelain dolls. They acted quite pridefully in their walk and conversations…or maybe these women just demonstrated a level of confidence that she hadn't felt in herself in quite some time. None of them seemed worried about showing so much skin or revealing too much of themselves. Some of them even held sticks in their mouths that blew out smoke. It smelt awful, almost like a burning house…

Even the men looked different; their hair was slicked back and shaped. They wore suits and shiny shoes. A lot of them wore hats as well. Most looked as though someone had pinched it in the middle. They looked so handsome…sl… "dapper", as she had heard someone say.

One day, I'm going to make a name for myself, right here, in this city.

The sun, though she couldn't quite see the horizon over the buildings, was going down. *Guess I should go back. Miss Hughes and the kids are expecting me.*

"Vanessa, we can never thank you for all of your hard work. There is no doubt that we will all miss you dearly, but after 23 years of being on the move, you need to grow some roots. Are you sure about New York City, though?"

"I am sure." Miss Hughes' gratitude and the smiles of the orphans warmed Vanessa's heart. Vanessa took just a few final moments to say goodbye to the children. As the train stopped, all but Vanessa and Miss Hughes involuntarily leaned. The movement of the train had become second nature to them after so many years.

Vanessa hopped off and waved as the new batch of kids joined Miss Hughes.

"Finally." Vanessa welcomed the industrial air as she took in a deep breath. "It's time to make my mark on this world."

Vanessa knew her goal, but she wasn't sure how to get there. She hadn't been able to use her magic much on the train. This was mainly due to her not knowing if someone would try to execute her again. Every so often, however, when the children would get really sick, Vanessa would heal them before they got worse or before the sickness would spread to the others. But other than that, she kept her magic to herself.

"Pardon me," a woman said when she turned around after bumping right into Vanessa.

"No trouble at all, really," Vanessa excused. She saw the woman's face up close. It was smooth and vibrant. Something sparkled and caught Vanessa's eye. "Such a beautiful ring."

"Oh, thank you. I got it from…"

The woman continued to tell her story while showing Vanessa the ring. Vanessa noticed that the woman's hand wrinkled with her gestures; they looked older than her face.

"Makeup," Vanessa inadvertently interrupted the woman's story.

"Excuse me?"

"Sorry. Nice ring. I must be going now." Vanessa left the woman very confused, but in that chance meeting, Vanessa had figured out what she wanted to do. "Makeup is my way of using my magic. All makeup does is cover up blemishes, like a bandage. But with magic, I can develop a makeup that actually helps people's skin look younger, or whatever their need is. They can hold on to their youth forever. Well, longer than what would be considered natural, let's say."

Vanessa continued to brainstorm as she wandered the streets. She didn't really have anywhere to go. *Maybe I'm getting ahead of myself.*

She walked up to what looked like a hotel. First things first.

Knock, Knock

A small door slid to the side, revealing a grated slat.

"Password?" a voice demanded.

"Sorry, what? I'm looking for a room."

"Use the front door." The slider shut in her face before she could apologize.

"Oh…" Vanessa hadn't realized that she was in an alley adjacent to the hotel. She walked to the front door and got a room for the night with gift money from Miss Hughes.

Why would you need a password to enter a building? Vanessa stood looking out her window. She could see the alley she had just left. People were going in and out of a door where she had just tried to enter. "I'm going to investigate."

She went back out through the lobby of the hotel, went outside, then stayed in the shadows. She was close enough to listen, but far enough away to stay hidden.

I can't be hearing that right, she thought, but gave it a go, anyway.

Knock, Knock.

"Password."

"Um…Coffin Varnish?"

The sliding door slammed shut again.

"I knew that couldn't–"

Then the door opened.

"Come on in."

"What rabbit hole did I just fall into?" she asked the well-dressed doorman. He didn't answer, but after looking around, she continued to say, "I guess I'm underdressed."

Vanessa winced as she pulled on the skirt of her simple, dark blue dress.

There was music; they called it jazz. It was flashy, yet relaxing at the same time. There was so much emotion on the musicians' faces as they blew into their brass instruments. The voice of the singer was strong and loud. People were dancing like it was their last night alive. Vanessa looked over at a mirrored wall with dim lighting. She walked over to a high table and sat on the circular chair.

"You aren't from around here, are you?" The woman next to her was leaning on her hand that was supported by her elbow on the table. She had a glass in her other hand.

"No, do I stick out that much?"

"Afraid so. I'm Shirley."

"Vanessa." They shook hands. "What is this place?"

"It's a speakeasy. Where did you come from?"

"I've been on the orphan train my whole life."

"That explains it."

"Is that…" Vanessa moved her head closer to Shirley and in a hushed tone asked, "alcohol?"

Shirley cackled with laughter. "Of course it is. That's why everyone is here. The prohibition has brought us all together. Isn't it luxurious? Want a drink?"

"Ummm…I guess so."

Shirley handed Vanessa a glass. It looked like clouded water. Vanessa took a sip.

"Oh, come on, drink up girl."

Vanessa giggled a bit, but did as she was told.

"There you go," Shirley said as she assisted in tipping the glass.

Vanessa could taste lemon and honey in it; of course, the lemon garnish helped pick that out. Besides those faint tastes, the alcohol was like a slap on the face. It burned a bit going down. Vanessa coughed some of it out towards the end of her gulp, but Shirley kept her hand against the glass, guiding it down Vanessa's throat.

"Let's go dance," Shirley said as she grabbed Vanessa's now empty glass and put it on the table, then dragged her out to the dance floor.

After a couple of songs, they went back to the bar.

"I feel fearless. I think I may fly…" Vanessa laughed.

"I know. Isn't it wonderful?" Shirley squealed. "Where are you staying tonight?"

"The hotel." Vanessa pointed up.

Shirley shook her head. "You're staying with me. Let's get your belongings, then we can head home."

Vanessa finished her second drink; Shirley had told her it was called a "Bee's Knees", then they exited the secret world.

The morning's warm rays woke Vanessa. She pushed the heavy fluffy covers off her and welcomed the light shining through the enormous windows.

"Ma'am." An older woman was standing in the doorway. "Miss Shirley is waiting for you downstairs. If you get dressed," the woman pointed to the laid out clothes on the portion of the bed that was still made and untouched by Vanessa's thrashing, "I can show you the way."

"Thank you. That'll be lovely."

The maid nodded her head a bit, then bowed out of the room, grabbing the double doors and closing them as she backed out.

The house was something out of dreams. The floors didn't move, which was a great plus for Vanessa, given her iron magic carpet for the past couple of decades. Intricately detailed molding joined walls and ceilings in each room. The staircase she descended hugged the rounded wall; her hand slid smoothly down the gold painted railing. She felt like royalty as she walked on the red carpet that led all the way to greet Shirley in a room with huge windows that let in the morning light and overlooked the tall green and golden-tipped grasses.

"I can't believe this is yours."

"For now, at least. I'm having a new place built a little way up the coast."

"Coast? There's a beach?" Vanessa ran to the window to see if she could see it.

"It's past the grass," Shirley laughed at her friend's child-like eagerness.

"Wow. How did you achieve all of this?"

"My family struck oil a decade ago, I got my allotment, and moved to the city. What can I say? We know how to spend humbly."

Vanessa huffed. *If this is humble, what was showy?*

"So last night, you told me about your business plan for a cosmetics store. I'm interested, but I have to say, I'm skeptical. You say you can make it really benefit the customers? I want to see it."

"No problem. Let me go grab something from my bag."

Shirley waved her to go ahead as she sipped her morning "juice". The only belongings Vanessa had were the flowers and herbs she had collected through her repetitive voyages across the country. She picked three plants, then ran back downstairs.

"I noticed your spots last night."

"Yes, well, I am older than you by…let's just say a few years."

Vanessa smiled and said to herself, "I highly doubt that." But told Shirley, "You look great."

"Yeah, yeah, what do you have for me?" As flattered by the compliment as she was, Shirley's focus was to see if Vanessa was crazy or not.

"This is ginseng and anise. This will help your skin return to its youthfulness."

"What's the other for?"

"Lavender." Vanessa held it up to her nose and took a deep breath in. "It smells good," she laughed, "but it also helps with anxiety and pretty much any other ailment you may have."

Vanessa mixed everything together in her hand, all the while concentrating. "Calm and unite." It had been a substantial amount of time since she had practiced. The faster she rubbed the flowers in her hands, the softer the ingredients got. Soon a liquid formed.

"May I see your arm?"

Shirley gave her the hand that was not responsible for bringing her "juice" to her lips. The warm serum absorbed into Shirley's skin.

"It smells divine," Shirley complimented with more interest as she finally set her glass down.

"Alright, take a look." Vanessa's heart was racing. She had hoped that even with being a little rusty, she had had enough lifetimes to practice, and she'd be able to just pick it back up. Vanessa bit her bottom lip as she waited for Shirley to react.

"My arm, it's like new…fully rejuvenated. How did you—?"

"I have my ways." Vanessa shrugged like it was no big deal, but the butterflies in her stomach were still flying frantically.

Shirley admired and compared her arm to the other. The serum felt soft to the touch with the zing of energy which was only intensified by the soothing scent. She had wanted to do something on her own. Have something that wasn't part of the "family money", but she had never known how to make her mark. Until now.

I want to invest in you, Vanessa. I'll get you all set up with a location, start-up costs, and help you with the business side of things. All you have to do is concentrate on working your magic."

Vanessa froze and looked at Shirley with astonishment, and a bit of fear and hesitation. Images of her recent past life were picking at her brain.

Shirley held out her other arm for Vanessa to restore, completely oblivious to Vanessa's reaction.

"Oh, right, the cosmetic magic." Vanessa relaxed again once she realized what Shirley had meant. "That's great! I promise to repay every cent."

"Of course, you will."

"I was wondering…"

"Spit it out then." Shirley was admiring her two smooth arms.

"May I add a speakeasy into the mix?" Vanessa held her breath, expecting the worst.

"Oh, honey, that's a given. And please stay here until you get on your feet, which I do not foresee taking much time at all."

Shirley was now rubbing her cheeks against her arms, like a cat greeting its owner, amazed at the smoothness.

Shirley took Vanessa under her wing. As Vanessa's benefactor, Shirley made sure that Vanessa could dress for any occasion. Vanessa's new bedroom had a walk-in closet that was filled with dresses from sexy to elegant. Shirley also threw in a few pricey pieces of jewelry to ordain

Vanessa's body and ensured they matched her new wardrobe.

Vanessa found the perfect location for her business, and with Shirley backing her financially as a partner, they didn't skimp on any details. They kept the store clean and simple, though still inviting to the public. Once customers came in and sampled the inventory, Vanessa's products practically sold themselves. When closing time approached, the focus turned to the dazzling life of the speakeasy. Vanessa made the password "lemons and sugar", something that she thought would help keep her grounded, reminding her to stay balanced.

Unfortunately, her sudden rise in class blinded her from where she started. Beauty and fashion made her vain and made her forget to help those in need, besides the needs of beauty.

"Oh dear, I know just what you need," Vanessa stated as she grimaced at the hag who had just entered the shop. "This is rosemary, maidenhair fern, and lavender. Rub into your hairs, those that you have left, and onto your scalp. Those grays will vanish right before your eyes, and you won't be missing any more either. That'll be twenty-five cents."

"I just wanted some perfume."

"No problem. I'll just add this jasmine perfume to your order. Thirty-five cents, please."

"Humph." The disgruntled woman walked out of the store empty-handed.

Vanessa watched her leave, and at the same time, saw the birds sitting on her shop's windowsill. "Wretched beasts," Vanessa said shrewdly.

The woman spun around to look at Vanessa. "I won't be returning," the woman said, then stormed out of the shop.

"I wonder what's wrong with her?" Vanessa said obtusely.

Vanessa met up with Shirley down in their hideaway after the store had closed for the day.

"I believe I'll be all paid up now," Vanessa mentioned as she sat at Shirley's table.

"Right, you are, darling, and I have a gift for you to celebrate. My house is finished—remember the new one I told you about when we first discussed our business plan?"

"How marvelous!"

"Indeed. I am gifting you my, our, well…your house…free of charge with the friend discount," Shirley said with a wink. "You'll have it all to yourself now, and I'll just be up the road a bit. You can visit anytime you wish."

"Are you sure? That is quite a gift! How can I ever repay you for everything?"

"After handing me that last repayment," both of the women laughed as Vanessa handed over the envelope with the cash in it, "Consider yourself debt-free. We are now strictly friends. You now have all profits for yourself to do with as you wish…and a castle at your disposal. Cheers." The two women clinked their glasses and sipped on their drinks.

"In that case, I'll throw a party in your honor before you move to your new house. Saturday night, alright?"

"Sounds smashing." They pressed their glasses to their painted lips, tilted their heads back, and reveled in the empire they had built.

"You've outdone yourself, Vanessa, dear."

"You are too kind. I'm going to get changed before the guests arrive." Vanessa made her way up her staircase and took off her lounge clothes. She looked at her bare, marked body in her long mirror. No matter what serum she concocted, nothing would take her scars away, at least not for longer than a few hours.

The sparrow perched on the balcony railing.

"For someone who wishes me a grand life, I sure have a lot of battle scars." It was the first time Vanessa had spoken to her mother in a long while. "You know, I wondered about you a lot growing up. Did you love me? Why did you leave? Would we ever meet, and if so, would you like me? Be proud of who I am? I honestly believe you'd answer all of those questions correctly in hindsight. That's not what is upsetting to me, though. I don't really care about the gift itself, it has been quite the journey seeing the world change. The reason I'm so pissed off is how you could care so little about the world you have me revisiting time after time."

Vanessa stood far enough inside to stay hidden from the arriving guests, but close enough to view them as they came into the courtyard.

"It amazes me…the glaze they all have over their eyes, preventing them from noticing the pain in their neighbors' lives." Vanessa walked over to her closet. She reflected on her behavior earlier with the older woman in her shop. "I fear even I have absorbed the self-centered tendencies, that of the humans and of you. I mean, I look in my closet full of clothes that I have never even dreamed of having and yet, I feel as though I have nothing to wear." She turned around to face her mother, but the sparrow had left…leaving Vanessa alone once again.

"Figures, you only want to be around to torment me, not to hear me rant on about how I'm actually feeling."

There was a dress splayed out on the bed with a note:

My deepest regrets.

Love, S

Vanessa tried the dress on.

The green shimmering gown hugged her body, accentuating her curves and highlighting her figure. She stood once again and faced the mirror. Her flaws vanished right before her eyes, and she admired how beautiful she looked.

"Thanks for the magical dress, and making me feel pretty for a night, but this alone won't make up for the fact that you are sucking the kindness out of the world."

Vanessa heard flapping close to her, as if it were in the room. "Did you decide to come back, Mother?" She turned around facing the open balcony.

"Oh. It's you. It's been so long. Last time was..." Vanessa stroked her scarred neck. "Well, you know."

The blue jay invited itself in and settled right on Vanessa's vanity.

Vanessa admired her dress some more. The v-neck line was perfect. The beading and dark green color made her eyes jump out more than they ever had. She was trying her darndest to be nonchalant about the piercing eyes of her sister, but she was very wary of her menacing presence.

So, Vanessa continued to babble, "You know, I can't say I've missed you or mother, but it's not like I really have a say in the matter, do I? There's no point in caring about life or anyone, for that matter. We'll all be here thousands of years down the road. You guys are going to do whatever you like. I might as well too, I guess."

An iridescent glow emerged from the bird.

"Must you always be so flashy when you do that?" Vanessa argued.

"It's in my nature," Lillian said unapologetically. "I want to offer an olive branch."

"Why should I trust you? The first time we met ended in my doom."

"I was just the messenger that time."

"I doubt you were one-hundred percent innocent."

Lillian shrugged her shoulders, her fairy wings moving up and down with them. "These would look great with your dress. Go on, take them." She held out emerald and gold earrings.

"This was part of Mother's olive branch… like the dress."

"Yes…I know."

Truthfully, Lillian had been observing Vanessa and Selena for some time now. Lillian hated the fact that Selena seemed to care for Vanessa more than her. *I mean, she's a human…a witch. She doesn't even carry the fairy bloodline, and yet, Vanessa is more important than I am?* Lillian had been stewing about how horrid Vanessa was treating their mother, even after she gave her the gift of life…many lives, in fact. And as far as Lillian was concerned, Vanessa did not deserve it.

"There's a way out, you know. A way to break the cycle," Lillian taunted her sister.

Vanessa stopped painting her face and searched Lillian's ocean blue eyes for a tell.

"What do you mean? Mother never mentioned a way for it all to end."

"Why would she? You know how selfish she can be." Lillian almost gagged at saying something so horrid about her mother, but she managed to keep her composure. Lillian watched as her sister struggled with herself.

Vanessa, although rather pensive with this possible new information, thought, *Should I break down and ask how to get out of this curse? She is a dark fairy, afterall Does she have an ulterior motive? Why didn't Mother tell me? Am I really ready for it all to end?*

"I think I'll join the festivities downstairs…give you some time to think." Lillian shined her light again, but this time, she simply hid her wings and changed her clothes.

Always the spectacle. Vanessa noted and shook her head. She stood and faced Lillian. "No—wait. I want to know."

Lillian grinned. She wanted to get rid of Vanessa once and for all so she could be number one, the way it should have been from the very beginning. "Your misery can cease by simply taking off your necklace."

"Then what? What happens exactly?"

Lillian wasn't sure, but she went with what sounded good, "You wait until your eventual death comes, and that's it."

"I just die…no coming back?"

"Yup," Lillian said with a pop of her lips.

Vanessa looked in her mirror again, caressing her butterfly necklace. The stones, her mother, and her life would all be done. I could restore happiness to this world and the people who inhabit it. Vanessa raised the necklace over her head.

Lillian's heart fluttered as fast as her wings do while flying. *I'll finally be mom's favorite.*

"I think—," Vanessa paused, then repositioned the pendant back in the center of her chest. "I want one more life." She walked to her closet and picked out a sheer black shawl.

Lillian's cloud-nine moment burst like a floating bubble. "What the hell for?"

"Love." Vanessa walked over to her balcony overlooking the joyous crowd below her.

Lillian admired her sister's gown and the flow of the shawl in the light breeze. "Ironic how it looks as though you have wings in your outfit."

Vanessa continued to watch the couples dance, kiss, and hold hands below her. She waved as Shirly made eye contact with her, holding up a champagne glass as a toast to their friendship and business. "What did you say?"

"Nothing, no need to worry your pretty, little, human head," Lillian snapped.

Vanessa didn't pay Lillian any mind, she just kept babbling about love. "I want love. This is my fourth life and yet I have never loved or been loved in a romantic way."

"It's a silly emotion, really. It's not a necessity to live…or die. Just end it now, and you can give the necklace to me." Lillian quietly advanced to her sister.

"Why do you care if I wait? I want love before I die." Vanessa finally turned toward her sister.

"Because," Lillian lunged, "you are stealing my spotlight, you insignificant witch."

Vanessa bent down, dodging Lillian's attack. Vanessa ran towards her bedroom door.

"You are ungrateful, weak, and, above all…human!" Lillian's shriek broke the light bulb in the room. She stepped on Vanessa's trailing dress, stopping her dead in her tracks. Lillian sped over to her, catching Vanessa's throat in her arm. Lillian raised her finger, ejecting her nail.

"You better put that toothpick away before I break it." Vanessa focused her energy the best she could, gasping for air at the same time. Vanessa finally snapped the nail. Lillian cried out again as pain shocked throughout her body, and she released her grip around Vanessa's neck.

"Let me have one more life, then I'll let go."

"No. No. No. You've had enough of Mother's time! It's my turn!"

Lillian spun like a tornado, changing back to her stronger fairy form. Like lightning, she charged for Vanessa again.

"You have a weak bloodline, sis. I will always win."

Lillian pushed her sister but not before grabbing for the necklace again. She missed it and instead watched as Vanessa toppled over the wooden rail of the balcony. She soared down, her dress' wings failing her. It was oddly peaceful for Vanessa. She was now curious about love, but was it really needed? Was it better to have never loved?

Vanessa saw her sister's angry face turning back into a bird. She failed to grab the necklace, but once again succeeded in killing her sister. Shirley, who heard the commotion and saw Vanessa falling, ran over from the crowd to be near her friend.

"Don't leave me," Shirley pleaded.

Vanessa felt Shirley embracing her hands. Blood seeped down her back, soaking her dress. She had slammed her head on the marble steps that led down to the courtyard.

"I'm afraid I have little choice in the matter, my friend." All Vanessa could do was attempt to laugh, but the taste of blood spitting out of her mouth choked then stifled her laughter.

"The lights are beautiful," Vanessa whispered. She looked at her dear friend's grief-stricken face as the darkness tookVanessa once again, but this time, the possibility of love lingered and gave her a flicker of hope or what was to come.

WWII

"I thought we talked about waiting for a boy?" Jon was being dragged by his wife up the steps to the nursery of St. Agnes Hospital.

"I know," Grace said. She stopped on the landing and looked up at him. "But this little girl has been there for a week now. She needs a home. Can you just come look at her?" Grace turned to continue dragging her husband up the stairs again. Then she stopped again and looked at him with a smile that looked like a little girl asking her parents for a cookie. "You should hold her, too." Grace then proceeded up the steps.

"We'll see," he said, then groaned as his body jerked backwards with the sudden movement forward aided by his wife.

They surrounded the little girl, lying in her bassinet. She looked so peaceful. Her big green eyes were begging for Grace and Jon to take her home.

Grace sneaked a peek at Jon, who was beaming from ear to ear. "She's so little," he said. He reached down and cradled the baby in his arms.

"What's the necklace for?" he asked his wife as he bounced his body, rocking the baby girl.

"No one knows, but she seems pretty attached to it."

Just as Grace said that, the baby started gnawing on a wing.

"I have a name picked out for you…" he said to the baby in a sort of tune.

"Vanessa," the couple said in unison.

Grace's face lit up. "So, we can keep her?"

"Absolutely," he said tenderly.

Once the paperwork was finalized, Jon and Grace, the doctor and nurse couple, brought baby Vanessa home.

Knock, Knock

"Time to wake up, sleepyhead. Breakfast is waiting."

Vanessa rose like a zombie with wisps of hair poking out of her braid, creating a lion's mane. She rubbed her eyes, then scooted her bum off the bed and looked toward her window. The sun was trying to shine through the curtains.

"Here, let me help you shine bright," Vanessa said as she drew open the curtains, basking in the morning's glow.

She looked out her window across the street and noticed a moving van. Two big guys were unloading a table. She couldn't see who the family was, but figured her mom would want to bring them an apple pie once they settled in.

Vanessa shifted her gaze to the yard. There had been a bunny there every morning for a week, nibbling on the grass. This time, however, the bunny was absent. A fluttering of feathers soon obstructed Vanessa's view. Her eyes followed the flurry of feathers to the fence. After she rubbed her still sleepy eyes, she squinted as she pressed her forehead on the window's glass.

"Those stupid animals."

Vanessa banged on the window a time or two, but the birds weren't budging. Vanessa threw open her bedroom door—not caring that it slammed against the wall—causing a picture to tilt. She ran down the stairs and passed her parents.

"Oh, good, you made it down." By the time Grace turned around to put flapjacks on the table, Vanessa had run out the back door, making the blinds rock back and forth and the screen door to slam shut.

Vanessa picked up some rocks from their garden and started throwing them at the wretched birds.

"How dare you come here. Go away."

The sparrow and the blue jay just sat there.

"You must think this is funny. Just because I'm 9 years old doesn't mean I don't remember how mean you are. Just leave me alone."

She went to throw another rock, but she had run out. The birds stayed glued to the fence. Vanessa crumpled, the dewy grass lightly poking her calves. She watched her tears bead on her thigh and soak into her shorts. She could still feel the unwavering stare of the birds on her, but she didn't care anymore.

"Are you okay?"

Vanessa raised her wet face to see a stranger on the other side of the fence staring at her as well. He was hanging over the fence. He had to have been on his tiptoes to see over.

"No."

"What's the matter?"

"Those birds."

"They are just sitting there."

Vanessa stood deliberately and stomped her foot. She furrowed her eyebrows and felt her nails dig into her palms.

"Birds are gross. They spread diseases and…well…they are just mean."

"Hey…hey…OK…I was just asking." The boy threw his hands in the air like an innocent bystander, which he was, and dropped back to the ground. All Vanessa could see were his eyes and hands now.

She giggled at him.

"What's so funny?" He picked himself up onto the fence again.

"You," Vanessa giggled.

The boy's eyes narrowed a bit, but raised with the smile she sensed he had.

He jumped down again, then ran to the side where the birds were and flew his arms up.

"Ahhhh," he shouted.

The birds took off.

Vanessa walked over to him.

"Thank you."

"My pleasure." He placed one hand on his stomach, and outstretched the other to his side, then lowered his torso in a formal bow. Once he was upright, he said, "I'm James. James Wilson."

"Nice to meet you." Vanessa picked up her imaginary dress and curtsied. "I'm Vanessa."

They stood there, making sure eye contact didn't linger for too long. Both looked down at the grass after a second or two.

"I just moved—"

"I haven't seen you—"

They giggled as they had spoken at the same time.

James didn't speak, but looked at Vanessa, inviting her to continue first.

Vanessa cleared her throat, then repeated, "I haven't seen you around before."

"Yeah, I'm moving in across the street."

"That's wonderful. Maybe we can be friends." Vanessa looked down at her bare feet. She had forgotten she was still in her pajamas. A rosy color rose to her cheeks.

"My first day here, and I already have a new friend. Aren't I lucky?"

"James." His mom called him from across the way.

"I guess I should go. When will I see you again?"

"Soon. Don't worry, my mom will want to welcome you with pie as soon as possible."

"Mmm, yummy, can't wait." James started running across her lawn towards the street.

"Thank you," Vanessa screamed, cupping the sides of her mouth.

"For?" James looked back at her.

"The birds."

He shrugged and glared as the sun was slightly in his eyes. "That's what friends are for. My favorite pie is apple." He looked up and down the street, looked back at Vanessa once more to wave, then crossed.

Vanessa waved back, then skipped to her house. Her mom opened the screen door. "There you are! I've been looking everywhere for you. What are you doing, child?"

"Just meeting the neighbor boy."

"I bet you left a great first impression, my dear." Mom tried not to smile. "Why don't you go get dressed, and do something with that bird's nest on top of your head, then come downstairs for some flapjacks and orange juice? The flapjacks are cold now, but you need to eat something."

Vanessa ignored the bird's nest comment and hurried up the stairs.

Rainbows graced the bright blue sky. All of her friends were there: Tristan, Cristina, Millie, and Shirley. All were sitting on blankets having a picnic. Butterflies danced amongst the full flowers, and her beloved caretakers, Lucian, Mama Helen, and Miss Hughes, greeted her. There were no birds in sight.

But then, an ominous storm cloud covered the poetic scene, and swarms of feathery fowl blew in with it, but two of the birds stood out. A brilliant light sliced through the darkness, and when Vanessa refocused, she saw her mother and sister.

"I took the darkness away for you, dear," Selena said.

Vanessa looked around. "You're the one who brought it here in the first place, and you took my family in the process." Her loved ones were nowhere to be found.

Selena corrected her daughter. "They aren't your family…we are."

Lillian and Selena advanced on Vanessa from the skies. Lillian swooped down and picked up Vanessa like a predator on its prey. They soared up towards the heavens, then Lillian stretched out her nail, and threatened, "You belong with the humans." She cut Vanessa's throat and watched her fall to her death.

Vanessa bolted up from her sleep, her hair stuck to her sweaty, glistening face. "Every damn night." Vanessa had a gut-wrenching feeling. She ran to her window and saw her sister in her hellacious pixie form.

Lillian grinned at her tormented sister and waved with her fingers.

Vanessa opened her window and reached out to hit Lillian. Vanessa underestimated her arm's reach and wobbled. Lillian stuck out her tongue, then cackled, mocking her sister's near death experience.

"Buzz off, you flying demon. And stop messing with my mind," Vanessa scolded.

Lillian flew off into the still, starry sky.

Vanessa sat on the edge of her bed. She could see herself in the mirror. She touched her neck where the scar from Lillian used to be, but no longer lived.

She heard the flapping of wings again. After glancing at her window, too tired to walk to her window, she noticed it was her mother this time.

"Oh goodie, two birds in one night. How lucky I must be. Can you change? I need to talk to you."

Without hesitation, Selena showed herself, all too happy to have a conversation with her daughter.

"Don't get too excited. I have a request and a question. After that, I want my space back."

Selena stood in silence, but nodded, showing she not only understood Vanessa's terms, but also respected them.

"My request is for you to keep Lillian away from me for this lifetime. She has killed me twice now. I know I can thank you for the first time, but the other was all on her own...right?"

"Yes, it was, and I know... She has been sneaking off at night, so I followed her this time. I swear I didn't know she was dusting your dreams. I'm sorry."

"I don't want to hear your apology. Just keep her away from me."

"I will, I promise."

"Yeah, whatever. My question is about my scars. I don't have any of them this time around. Why?"

"The dress I gave you...you were wearing it that night..."

"Yeah, trust me, I know that part. What does the dress have to do with anything?"

"Well, it removed your scars that night. That's why I gave it to you. I enchanted it to heal you. Since you died in it, you died without scars; therefore, you reanimated without them."

"Interesting..." Vanessa looked back at her neck in the mirror. She almost smiled at her mom, but she stopped herself and dismissed her mother. "Alright. You can leave now. I have school in a few hours."

Selena looked at her daughter, craving her love and forgiveness.

"Vanessa, I am sorry. I just wanted time with you. I…"

"I said you can leave," Vanessa demanded. Her heart raced, pounding hard in her chest. She clenched her jaw together so tight she tasted the iron in her blood from biting her cheek. And yet, her eyes welled up as she remembered all the loss this "gift" had brought her.

Selena bowed her head, but before she fully returned to her sparrow form, a single teardrop fell and absorbed into the floor. "I love you, Vanessa," she whispered. Vanessa closed the door right after Selena's wings left the room.

Vanessa stood, books in hand, at the edge of her sidewalk. The air smelled fresh. She marveled at how much she enjoyed the spring, even though she had seen so many.

"Good morning, James," Vanessa greeted as she waited for him to come around to the passenger side of the car.

"Morning, Vanessa." He kissed her on the cheek, then opened her door.

They sat for a while with no conversation, just listened to "Boogie Woogie Bugle Boy" by The Andrews Sisters.

Vanessa tapped her foot to the swinging beat, but noticed that James wasn't doing his typical head bob.

"Everything alright, James? You seem a bit distracted."

"Um, yeah." He kept his eyes on the road.

"That seemed convincing," Vanessa snarked.

"What? Oh…I'm sorry, Vanessa. I…I need to talk to you, but I don't want to do it before your classes. You need to focus. Let's get together for lunch. I can meet up with you after your second class. OK?"

"Sounds dandy, but you are alright, right?"

"As long as you're my friend, I am." He faced her with a smile, which she returned.

James pulled up to the campus. "Have a good morning, and I'll meet you in our normal place."

"Thanks for the lift, James. I'll see you then."

When class finished, Vanessa gathered her notebooks. Words like "abscess" and "contusion", "fractures" and "sutures" fried her brain. She ran out to the courtyard to meet James under the recently bloomed cherry tree. James was already sitting on the bench. He was hunched over with his head resting in his hand, covering his eyes. She went up behind him and rested her hand on his shoulder.

"James, it's time to spit it out. Something is wrong. Please tell me what's troubling you. Friends don't keep secrets."

"Come sit, Vanessa."

She sat down, and he took her hands.

"James, you're scaring me."

"Vanessa, it's my turn. I dropped out of school to join the war. I leave tomorrow."

As his eyes sank to face their clasped hands, Vanessa's heart sank too. She felt as though she was going to throw-up.

"We knew it was coming, I suppose. You're so close to finishing school, I guess I just thought you'd see it through," she said.

"That was the plan, but I can't take it anymore. How can I sit in a classroom while others are dying?" he finished.

Every single time I get close to someone… She remembered all of her family and friends she had loved…and lost… through the centuries. *I have watched them leave, or I would die before I could really have some time with them.*

Vanessa brushed her tears aside, reaffirmed her grip with James' hands, and stared right into his eyes. "We will get through this. We can write letters, and I was planning on volunteering as a nurse as soon as I finish with school. I can do summer courses instead of waiting for fall, and I'll be there in a jiffy after the Army's training course."

Vanessa wanted to protect him, but at the same time, she didn't know how that spell would work on someone other than herself. The only protection spell she had used was the one that kept her completely hidden from the world around her. If he disappeared, then he would let down the men whom he was supposed to protect. *If I don't know the risk, I shouldn't do the magic,* she convinced herself. But she still fought a tugging feeling in her heart.

"Sounds like a plan," James said. He tucked a loose strand of her hair behind her ear. Vanessa nestled her cheek against his warm touch.

Her sickened feeling turned into something she had never felt before. It felt like bees buzzing around after a bear stole their honey. She promptly stood up—her hands shook, and her face was flushed.

"I have to go to the hospital. My rotation starts soon."

James stood and stepped towards her. He got confused when she backed up.

Vanessa reached for the books she had left sitting on the bench. She ensured to keep plenty of space between her and James. Then she brushed past him.

"Will I see you before I go?"

"Of course." She ran back to him. "We are friends for life." Vanessa awkwardly and cautiously leaned in to give him a peck on the cheek. Their eyes met for a second, though it felt like one of her lifetimes had gone by. Then she rushed to the hospital. *What am I feeling? Is this purely a worry for my dearest friend leaving for the war, or is this something bigger?*

Clouds covered the vast sky so close it made it seem like it was almost possible to touch them. The weather hadn't called for sun that day, making the already sorrowful day much more gloomy.

"I can't believe you're leaving." Vanessa stood next to James, both of whom were facing the empty train tracks, waiting for the train to steal him away.

"Vanessa…" James closed his eyes and sucked in the biggest breath ever, searching for the words. "I did some thinking last night, after our talk." James took her hands and faced her.

She waited, eyes open wide. She smiled at him, even though they were red and puffy from the obvious crying.

"Vanessa, I—"

Whoo, Whoo

His voice was drowned out by the arrival of the train. Vanessa pulled away from James to shield her eyes from the smoke and soot the engine produced.

"I can't hear you," she yelled. "What did you say?"

The train stopped after blowing its whistle again. James shook his head. "I'll tell you the next time I see you…which will be soon."

Vanessa didn't think she had any more tears left, and yet they flowed freely from her emerald eyes. She glued herself to his chest, burying herself in his embrace. James felt her body relax into his as he encased her with his arms.

"All aboard," the conductor boomed.

Vanessa released her hold of him. "I will see you soon, I promise."

He threw his sack onto one of the train cars, then hoisted himself up. He waved farewell as the train pulled away from the station.

Vanessa didn't move from her spot until the train was out of sight.

Dear Vanessa,

I'm sorry this is the first I've been able to write. We don't get a lot of downtime here. Vanessa, I had no idea what it was going to be like over here, but now that I am here, I'm terrified. The wounded count is high, and there never seems to be enough supplies to go around. Death is vividly real here. It's dark and hateful. The sad part is we are fighting people who are as terrified as we are. I have killed people, Vanessa. It breaks my spirit and haunts my sleep. I know you are headstrong, but I am begging you to help by staying over there. Do not come to this world. It'll change you in ways you won't recognize.

Your Friend,
J. Wilson

Vanessa had just run home from her last exam to search the mailbox for a letter from James. After reading his words, she burst into tears. "This hate, this war…it wouldn't even be a factor if I wasn't alive. My life caused this turmoil. How can I not go?" She ran up the stairs to her bedroom and grabbed paper and pen.

> *Dear James,*
>
> *You care for me unlike anyone I have ever met, but James, I cannot…I will not stand idly by and simply pray that the war will end. I am trained in healing people. It is my duty to help in any way I can.*
>
> *James, I should have said this to you before you left, but I wasn't sure of what I was feeling. There is no doubt in my mind now. I love you, James Wilson. You better believe I'm going to see you again as soon as I finish my training. Don't you dare leave me here alone.*
>
> *Love,*
> *Vanessa*

Summer classes seemed to go by as fast as pouring molasses into cookie batter. Every day Vanessa checked the mail. Weeks had gone by with not one letter in sight. She sat on her porch steps, fidgeting with her necklace, as always. *Did I ruin our friendship by telling him I love him? Did he die?* Her stomach churned at the thought.

Vanessa left on orders right after the Army training course, which ended mid-fall. She was to be based at a portable surgical unit.

Vanessa jumped at the opportunity to help the next wave of wounded even though casualties flowed in without rest just a couple of weeks into her deployment.

"Sir, are you hurt?" another staff member asked a soldier.

"No. I'm here with some members of my unit who are wounded."

That voice. Vanessa knew it all too well.

"James?" She looked over the crowd of injured. "James!" Vanessa spotted him and wedged her way through the tight quarters.

"Vanessa?" James stepped forward, and with open arms, picked her up. Dirt covered his face, but his hazel eyes broke through all the grime. She saw pain in them; he was tired and seemed to have lost his vitality…his hope.

"It's bittersweet seeing you here, Vanessa. I hate that you are here." He looked around. The wounded were everywhere—some hadn't eaten in days, some no longer had all of their limbs, and some were covered head to toe with a blanket. "But I can't say I haven't missed you."

Vanessa could feel his pulse race with her head resting on his chest. She wondered if he could feel hers as well.

"Nurse…Nurse!"

"I have to go. Don't leave though…" She reluctantly pulled away.

"I won't. I plan on staying the night at least."

"Alright," she yelled over the chaos.

Vanessa stepped over patients in search of James, but stopped when a soldier grabbed her ankle.

"Nurse."

"I'm here. How can I help?"

"It hurts," the soldier moaned.

"What's your name?"

"Daniel."

"Daniel, I'm going to look at your dressing and see what I can do, okay?"

Vanessa noted his shortness of breath, then looked at his thigh wound. Everything seemed fine; the stitches were clean, no unusual redness. She couldn't see why he would be in so much pain.

"Where does it hurt, Daniel?"

Daniel grasped his stomach. Vanessa moved up to his torso. In doing so, she stepped into a puddle.

"Sorry, I couldn't move because of the pain, but I couldn't hold it anymore."

"I understand, Daniel. No need to be ashamed or apologize."

Vanessa noticed the liquid had stained her shoes. It was red.

"Daniel, did the doctors inspect your abdomen?"

He shook his head.

Vanessa lifted his shirt; his stomach looked as if someone had kicked him a thousand times over. She looked over the sea of injured around her. There was no quick way out, and by the look of his current state—the blood in the urine and pain and bruising around his stomach—the leak in his abdomen had been there for quite some time now. That meant his likelihood of making it through surgery, let alone getting there, was slim to none.

"Daniel," Vanessa whispered into his ear. "I need you to help me, alright?"

He looked at Vanessa with the little energy he had, almost pleading for her to put him out of his misery.

"I need you to close your eyes, and trust me. This might pinch a bit, but I'm going to help you. Can you do that for me?"

Daniel didn't have the strength to worry anymore, but a steady stream of tears flowed from his eyes. He closed them, and then Vanessa closed hers.

"Calm and unite, calm and unite." She placed her hands on Daniel's battered stomach. He twitched some, but otherwise stayed quiet and relaxed.

Vanessa released his stomach, then wiped the tears from his eyes and dirty face. He looked up at her. This time, his eyes showed her a spark of relief and gratitude.

"Thank you, my guardian angel."

She returned the smile, then stood up and continued her quest to find James.

Vanessa finally found him in a secluded area away from the group with his buddies, whom he had come in with earlier. They were all eating. Vanessa had foregone her rations so the flood of wounded could gain the strength they needed in order to help them heal and return to battle if they were able.

"Did you already eat?" James asked.

Vanessa looked at him, and said a quick, "Yeah."

"You always were a horrible liar." James handed her some of his bread and water.

"Are you sure? You guys need it more than I do."

"Eat, Vanessa," he said as he shoved the food into her hands.

"Thank you," she responded with a big bite in her mouth.

"Do I want to know the last time you ate?"

She shook her head as she continued to shove the food and water into her body.

They sat there making pleasantries, then James asked, "Want to walk with me?"

"Of course." Vanessa's stomach started aching. *Was it the food or the fear of the upcoming conversation? They hadn't talked about the letter. Maybe he hadn't even received it.*

They ventured just a little way away from the rest of the camp, but still within "safe" parameters. It was actually where a lot of the medical staff slept…when they were able to sleep. A few of them were taking advantage of the brief pause in the wounded now. Vanessa and James could both use some shut eye as well, but they had been apart for far too long.

"James—"

"Vanessa—"

They chuckled.

"You first," James offered.

"I thought you had died or—"

"Or that I freaked out about your letter?"

Vanessa snapped her head to look at him. She could tell her stomach was in knots because of this discussion, not from the food. James smiled, but still faced forward on their walk, keeping a constant watch on their surroundings until he stopped. Now facing her, he picked up her hands.

"I got your letter, but they hit our supply helicopter when it was sending my letter out to you. Then we moved locations, and by that time, I wasn't sure if you were home or here. I knew you wouldn't stay away from the war. Your heart is just too big for that."

Vanessa felt dizzy as her body warmed even more in the already toasty environment. She swayed one way, but James centered her.

"Are you alright?"

"Yes…must be the heat…"

"Vanessa, the truth is…"

She felt as though she was going to be sick. She was hanging on to each word he said.

"I love you too. I should have said it at the train station, but I was too much of a coward to repeat it."

Vanessa pulled his head down to hers and kissed his chapped lips.

"You are no coward, PFC. James Wilson. I was scared too, I'm so glad—"

James touched his lips to hers again.

All anxiety, pain, and thoughts about war, had disappeared in that moment as they melted into each other. The world spun around them, but for a split second, they were in the clouds.

WhooOOoo, WhooOOoo

What little lantern and flashlight they had was immediately turned off, and everyone splayed out on the ground. They spoke no words as the warning sounds blared into the night. Even after they stopped, the camp stayed still. The buzzing of planes overhead kept them to the ground. They had no way of knowing if they were friend or foe.

Vanessa and James lay there, their faces pressed against the dirt. They held hands and never looked away from one another. Vanessa thought the "blackouts" had been happening more frequently recently. The days seemed so long; she often wondered if it was ever going to end. But at this very moment, she only thought of James.

In the few heartbeats that passed as the planes overhead turned around, there was quiet—a false sense of safety. That's when she heard scurrying behind James' head. Vanessa moved her eyes and finally saw the creature's eyes reflecting off the moonlight. The faintest chirp released into the air, but Vanessa stayed frozen in her place next to James.

Don't even think about harming James just because you want me all to yourself. I'm entitled to one love story in my long, lonely life.

Though Vanessa didn't speak out loud, she knew the sparrow had heard her loud and clear.

Chirp it repeated, then took off.

Vanessa sighed in relief, then returned her attention to James, who was staring at her like the love-drunk soldier he was.

They remained on the ground for the rest of the night. Neither of them slept. They just breathed in each other's air, and relished in their short time together.

They gave the "all clear" earlier that morning, but restrictions on music and other loud recreations were implemented.

"I need to check on patients," Vanessa stated.

"Unfortunately, I have to head back out, but before I do…" James got down on one knee. "If I ever get time to sneak away from this war and visit you…will you marry me?"

They had an audience now. Nurses and patients alike circled around them and waited for Vanessa to respond.

"Yes! Of course I'll marry you."

He stood and picked her up, swinging her around. For once, she was taller than he was. She leaned over and kissed him as he set her down. When their lips released, she added, "That's what friends are for."

He chuckled and picked her up again. She rested her forehead on his.

"PFC Wilson, I hate to do this, but we need to move out."

"Understand, sir."

James set her down. "I'll see you soon, I promise." He kissed her once more and brushed a tear that had just fallen from Vanessa's eye. "I love you, Vanessa."

"I love you, too." She couldn't resist smiling at him.

James threw his bag on his back and headed to the exit, leaving Vanessa once again.

Dear Vanessa,

    They informed me we'll be back at your location in a few days for a supply pick up. We can get married then. I love you.

James

Vanessa did a little happy dance, but soon stopped when she noticed that some of her patients were playfully mocking her.

She only had to wait a couple more days.

That night, another air raid hit. The medical team hadn't yet finished with the victims from the day, so they broke regulations and did what they could in the dark instead of hunkering down. Vanessa did her secret rounds, making sure injuries weren't missed, and helping them if they had been overlooked. By daybreak, the nurses were collecting soiled clothing and various fabrics, doing their best to sterilize surgical tools and trying to get some sleep themselves. Their efforts were cut short, however, when the wounded arrived from the night's close call. Vanessa geared herself up and headed to the first victim to assess injuries.

This raid was bad, she thought. Many of the soldiers were past the point of saving. The chaplain made his rounds, granting last rites.

"Nurse Vanessa."

"Yes, Father?"

"This soldier is asking for you personally." Vanessa froze, her heart sinking into her stomach; chills ran up her spine as she feared what her mind already knew. She pushed her way to the chaplain like a plow in a snowstorm.

"James," she cried. She held his hand while looking over his mangled body. Blood was everywhere; there was no telling where it was coming from. "Oh my God, James." Vanessa cried uncontrollably, her body shaking with each sob. "James…I can fix this," she tried to whisper, but her emotions were too erratic to keep her in control.

"No, Vanessa," he strained.

"Yes, I can. I can heal you."

James looked at her dead in the eye. "I know," he said.

Strangely, Vanessa could tell he knew her secret, but how?

"I just knew, Vanessa. It doesn't matter now. I don't want you to heal me. I have lived my life. This is how it ends."

The chaplain started to depart, allowing them time together to say goodbye.

"Father," James' voice cracked; blood splattered as he coughed. "I don't want last rites. Just marry us, please."

Vanessa couldn't collect her thoughts and organize her feelings at the same time. Keeping the two separate seemed impossible at the moment. *Should I just heal him against his will…would that make me like my mother? What would the sacrifice be? Another's life? What about their loved ones? Could I live with myself, knowing that I took someone else's happiness? But what about my love?*

"If she'll still have me?" James interrupted her thoughts.

"Of course, I'll still marry you." She tried to collect herself.

"The quick version, Father, if you don't mind." James' voice was soft now. He continued to cough up blood each time he spoke.

"Right. Do you, Nurse Vanessa Ash, take Private First Class James Allen Wilson to have and to hold, for better or for worse, for richer or poorer, in sickness and in health, to love and cherish from this day forward until…" the Father hesitated. Vanessa was still trying to control her hysterics, knowing that this was the only day she'd be married to the love of her life. "death…do you part?"

"I do," Vanessa blubbered.

"And Private First Class James Allen Wilson, do you reciprocate those vows?"

"I do," he gargled. He tried clearing his throat, but his cough was too weak for the pool that was collecting. Vanessa shifted his body to the side, allowing the clog to flow out of his mouth.

"By the power vested in me, by God as our witness, I now pronounce you husband and wife."

Vanessa lowered her lips, gently touching his sticky red-stained lips, and kissed her true love.

The air raid sirens wailed once more. Normally, its daunting song echoed up Vanessa's spine, bringing goosebumps to her skin as her heart skipped a beat. But this time, though part of her heard the explosions and subsequent sirens, the only thing that mattered, the one thing she heard, was the sound of James' labored breathing. His ragged breaths were uneven as he fought for each lungful of air. Then he exhaled slowly, painfully. Nothing mattered but that next sweet lungful…*just a few more moments, please…*

Boom, Boom

Chaos manifested around the newly wedded couple as the bomb's new target was that of the hospital. The medical personnel did their best to corral the wounded, trying to escape death, but Vanessa couldn't leave James. She also knew that their efforts to escape were futile.

"Go," James breathed.

"Never, I'm going to stay with you, husband…till death do us part."

James knew not to argue with his powerful wife, nor did he have the energy to try.

"I…love…you," he mouthed.

Vanessa could barely hear him. His breathing became erratic.

Boom, Boom, Boom

"That's what friends are for," she stumbled over her words, her body involuntarily heaving from the crying, like skipping a stone on the water's surface.

With his last bit of strength, James grabbed Vanessa's hand and moved it to his chest, holding her close to his heart. He closed his eyes and breathed his last.

Vanessa laid her head down on James' body. She knew what was coming, and didn't pay any mind to the panicked birds next to her.

Boom

21st Century

A big red truck pulled into what looked like a large house. Selena waited for the people who had just arrived to enter the building before she tiptoed up to the door. With a flick of her wrist, a small vintage baby carriage appeared. Selena held baby Vanessa in her arms, trying to keep her calm. The baby seemed more upset this time around.

"I guess you really loved him. I am glad you found love; it is a wonderful feeling, isn't it? I felt it once, for your father. If only I could feel it again. I think my heart is too cold for me to allow anyone to get so close again. You, on the other hand, have another shot. I have watched these people for a while. You'll surely be in exceptional hands. I will always be here if you need me, and know that I do love you, my dear butterfly."

"That was a rough one," Brian Clark said as he pulled off his coveralls.

"That was nothing, rookie. Just you wait." One of the more senior firefighters shook his head at him as he wiped the smoke's soot from his face.

"Why don't you go ahead and start cleaning the engines?" Another guy threw a towel and a bucket at Brian.

"Yes, sir." Brian stood up from the breather he had been taking, and started sudsing the trucks.

Selena touched her forehead to the child's, then kissed her on the cheek. She then placed her daughter in the carriage. After looking around, she returned to her bird body and fluttered about the baby's head. The sound of the bird's wings and the rapid movements caused Vanessa to cry. Selena swooped up into a tree across the grassy front lawn and waited for her daughter's rescuer.

After hosing off the bubbles, Brian heard some cries…baby cries. He searched the engine bays, but didn't see anything. He went to the door and opened it to find a baby in a carriage. There was a note attached to the handle of the stroller.

Dear Firefighters,

I am not fi2t to properly care for this child. My hope is that one of you would care for her. I ask you to keep her name as Vanessa. You will see a burn scar on her chest over her heart. Please know that she was born with it. I did not do this to her, nor am I giving up my rights

as a parent because of this. I am simply not fit
to be a proper mother to her.

Sincerely,
S

Brian looked around to see if the mother was still close by, but he only saw a sparrow on the nearby tree branch. He picked up the child, who now seemed calm in his arms. Brian held the necklace in his hand, trying to distinguish any markings, but found none. He recognized the interesting burn scar that was mentioned in the letter. The scar not only lay over her heart, but also in the shape of the butterfly pendant itself.

Brian looked at the bird again. It was still standing there watching him. He got this feeling that this child was his responsibility now—not to give away, but to care and raise as his own.

"Rookie." The guys had returned to check on his progress with the washing.

Brian entered the engine bay; the firemen flocked to him like vultures to roadkill. Brain handed his chief the note. "I'm going to care for her."

While the other guys laughed, the chief saw the seriousness in Brian's stoic face. The chief responded with a simple, "Okay."

The guys stopped laughing and soon followed suit with their leader.

"We have your back, rookie," they agreed. "What's her name?"

Brian let the child grab his finger. He booped her in the nose with his free pinky. The baby giggled.

"Her name is Vanessa."

Beep, Beep, Beep

Vanessa sprang out of bed and looked for the door. It was closed. She splatted to the floor, then army-crawled to her second-story window. She quickly unlocked it and pushed it up with ease. Vanessa grabbed the collapsible ladder out from behind her bookshelf, then draped it over the window's edge. She waited for it to fully unravel before she swung her legs over the window's threshold, one at a time. She climbed down and ran to the mailbox at the end of their stretched out driveway.

"Morning, Vanessa."

A bit winded, she greeted the newspaper boy riding his bicycle. "Morning, Timmy."

"Another fire drill?" He circled around the cul-de-sac so he could continue his conversation with her.

"Yup. Dad will pop out of the bushes in three, two, one."

"Well done, Vanessa. That was a new record." Brian hugged her, then greeted Timmy.

"Hi, Mr. Clark," Timmy returned.

"Now…quiz time."

Vanessa's dad had no shame at the fact she was outside in her pajama pants and a ratty old t-shirt, with her hair all in a tussle. But she loved him for caring so much, and given her past experiences with fire, she was okay with the frequent fire safety reminders.

"What do you do if you get caught on fire?"

"Stop, drop, and roll," Timmy chimed in as he made another pass.

"I'm glad you listen to our monthly lessons, Timmy, but don't people need their newspapers?"

"Of course, sir." With Timmy's last drive-by, he winked at Vanessa, then stood on his pedals and sped away.

"Next question. When should we change the batteries in the smoke detectors?"

"I believe that's next week."

"No, no…we change them on daylight's saving time."

"Which is…" she hinted as she lifted her chin and eyebrows.

"Oh, right. Aren't you the clever one? I suppose that is next week. Huh. Anyway…"

Vanessa giggled at her dad.

"Question number three…"

Vanessa thought it funny he pretended to be the host on a game show every time they did the drills.

"What do you take with you when you hide in the closet because your exit door is on fire?"

"Trick question. 'Don't hide, go outside.' Never stay inside even if it's scary, and you shouldn't bring anything with you."

"And why is that?"

"Because we are not replaceable."

"How right you are. Alright, let's go get ready for school."

Vanessa headed back up to her room and kneeled down next to her bed. She pulled out a sketch pad.

"You are not replaceable," she repeated. She held a drawing she had created as soon as she was able. "James Wilson." It was a lifetime ago, but she still grieved the loss of her only love. "I should have died with him—taken this cursed thing off."

Vanessa almost yanked it off of her neck, but then thought of Brian, her dad. He was kind and truly loved her.

It was the first time she had felt even remotely normal, even despite the decently sized burn over her heart.

"How symbolic that this scar is over my heart. That is what hurt the most." She talked to the face on the parchment. "I won't find anyone else like you. You knew what I was and still loved me. You understood the balance of life and selflessly refused the opportunity to survive."

"Vanessa." Brian knocked. "Do you want pancakes and bacon, or waffles and bacon?"

Vanessa scrambled to hide the picture. She didn't think that her dad would find it appropriate for his teenage daughter to have some grown man's picture; it would certainly raise some questions.

"Waffles and bacon sounds good."

"And so it shall be."

Vanessa shook her head at Brian's attempts to sound royal.

"Finish getting ready, then come on downstairs. You don't want to be late for school."

Vanessa rolled her eyes at the thought of school. Everyone already thought she was a genius; they called her "wise beyond her years" and said she had an "old soul". If they only knew. She kissed the penciled memory, then returned it to its hiding place.

A glimmer of light caught her eye while she was brushing her hair in her ensuite bathroom. She opened the door more to find Lillian sorting through her closet.

"What the hell are you doing here? Are you trying to get caught? Or did you come to kill me again…you think the third time's a charm?"

"Don't be silly, Ness, but I thought we had an agreement. Though it seemed a tad short lived, you did find your love, nonetheless."

Vanessa all but gagged at the random nickname. "Yes…I did, but now I have Brian."

Lillian charged at the necklace, but as soon as she touched it, she bounced back and hit the wall behind her.

"What the—" Lillian stood and straightened out her outfit. Another glimmer of light floated its way in through the window.

"Oh goodie, a family reunion," Vanessa voiced with much sarcasm as she walked back into the bathroom.

"Vanessa, is everything alright?" Brian had heard the thud of Lillian crashing into the wall.

"Fine dad. I just dropped…myself." Vanessa hit her forehead with her palm.

What a stupid response. She did her best to explain her odd answer. "I stepped on my shoes next to my bed and fell."

"Okay, make sure you put those away. You don't want them to block an exit if a fire occurs."

"Yeah, got it." She shook her head again.

The girls waited until Brian's footsteps faded down the steps.

"Hello, Vanessa," Selena said with some shyness about her. She did her best to keep her distance from Vanessa, rather than pushing herself onto her daughter.

"Hello," Vanessa responded. She raised her eyebrow, noticing Selena's out of character timidness.

"Is there anything you need from me?" Selena asked

"Vanessa pushed me—"

Selena held up her hand and looked over her shoulder to glare at Lillian. Selena looked as if her head might explode in anger.

Lillian had her hands on her hips and was tapping her foot.

"I wasn't asking you, Lillian. I was asking Vanessa."

Vanessa stuck her tongue out at her sister while Selena's attention was still on Lillian, encouraging her to keep quiet.

"And you shouldn't lie, Lillian. I saw you reach for Vanessa's necklace. I placed a protection spell on it from you, since you seem to think that killing your sister is some sort of sport."

Lillian's mouth gaped open. When she stomped her foot, she transformed back into her bluejay form, fluttered about Vanessa's head, then zoomed out of the room in a huff.

"Thank you for the protection."

"You're welcome. Anything else I can do for you?"

Vanessa thought. It wasn't like she could tell her mom about her pact with Lillian. Selena would not want Vanessa to take the necklace off, either. And, it seemed, Selena had already taken care of the Lillian threat. Vanessa figured that since she could still touch it, that the protection spell wouldn't affect her taking it off when the time was right.

"No, I think that's all."

"Okay." Selena started walking towards the window. She placed her hand on the window's siding. "Vanessa?"

Vanessa popped her head out of the bathroom. "Yes?"

"Are you happy with Brian?"

"I am." Vanessa tilted her head and propped the door open so she could see Selena better. "Why do you ask?"

"I have mentioned before that I love you. I know you may not believe me, but it is the truth. But I'm glad you're happy, and I am terribly sorry for your most recent loss." She lowered her head. Without looking back at her daughter, Selena leaped off the sill.

Vanessa rushed to see if she had fallen, but soon, the sparrow rose towards the sky. "What a bizarre morning." She grabbed her bookbag and headed down the stairs for breakfast.

Vanessa walked around her classroom, inspecting the progress of her student-group research presentations. She had given each group a historical event to write about, then they were to present their findings in front of the entire class.

"Check those dates, Hannah. Prohibition was not in the 1940s. And Ken, the Salem Witch Trials are called that for a reason. Your location is off."

The bell rang for lunch, and within seconds, the students had spun out of the classroom like a tornado. Vanessa was picking up the loose papers that had fallen off the desks when she heard a knock at the door. She turned around, greeted by a vase of flowers that was hiding a man's face.

"Hello, Tim," Vanessa laughed.

"How'd you know it was me?" He peered out from behind the dozen red roses.

"I'd be stupid to think otherwise. You have given me a dozen roses on the anniversary of our first playdate since our first playdate anniversary when we were five years old."

"You can't blame a man for trying." Tim squirmed and finally placed the vase on her desk before he dropped them. "Vanessa." He pulled at his collar. "Would you want to go to dinner with me tonight?"

Vanessa sighed. Some of the air blew up her bangs. "Tim, I can't. I'm sorry."

The guy looked like a deflated basketball. His arms went lifeless at his sides as he scratched the back of his calf with his other foot.

Vanessa walked over to him. His head was still looking down at his loafers. "It's not because you aren't a good man or anything…because you are. You're kind, smart…" Vanessa picked up his chin, and rested her hand on his cheek, "…and crazy good-looking." She giggled at his puppy-dog eyes, but what she said, she meant. "I just don't think love is for me. People tend to get hurt."

Tim nodded, understanding that she had a wall up for some reason, but he wanted to respect that. "Well, I'll see you around, still? And, of course, this time next year." Tim winked and flashed her a sad smile.

"It's a date." Vanessa's eyes widened when she realized what she had just said. "Not like a date, date, but a date."

"I gotcha. Bye, Vanessa," he said as he turned to leave her classroom.

"Bye, Timmy."

The bell rang again, declaring the end of the school day. Miss Vanessa managed to leave the building before the children. They always seemed to take their time at their lockers talking with their friends as if talking as much as they did during her class wasn't enough. She got into her car and turned on the scanner she had bought in highschool.

"All available units, please respond to 13 Maple Rd. Medic unit, standby."

Vanessa put her car into gear, and sped out of the parking lot, almost cutting off the buses. She saw the smoke above the houses. She turned the corner and parked on the side of the street. Vanessa ran the couple of blocks to the address that she heard on the scanner. She snuck into the backyard while the family and all the commotion were happening out front.

"Calm and unite." Vanessa combined what Lucian and Mama Helen had taught her. She drew water from the grass, flowers, and the family's garden pond, and united her mind, body, and heart. She was stronger than ever. The water shot through the already broken glass of the home's windows. Vanessa maneuvered the water so it could douse the bigger areas with flames. Vanessa double-checked the house—leaving a small flame or two so it didn't seem odd that all the fire had suddenly disappeared—then let the fire department finish the job.

Vanessa jumped back over the gate and headed to her apartment.

After some time had passed, Vanessa gave her dad a call.

"Hey dad, how was your day? Anything exciting?"

"Not really exciting, but we had a house fire down on Maple."

"You don't say? Do you know how it started? Were there any casualties?" Vanessa walked around her small kitchen island while she ate some cheese and grapes.

"It started with a cigarette. The man fell asleep. He has some burns, but not as bad as it could have been. He had been drinking, so he didn't wake up right away. The fire ended up not being as bad as what we were expecting."

"Well, I'm glad it turned out well." She beamed and patted herself on the back, literally. This is what she looked forward to—helping her dad, who was now the fire chief, put out fires by using her magic.

Vanessa arrived at her classroom. "The calm before the storm," she said as she flicked on the lights. She set her coffee on her desk, then began laying out papers on each little desk. It was time for a pop quiz.

"Vanessa, have you seen the news?" Mrs. Ritters was so hysterical that Vanessa could barely make out what she said.

"No, what happened?" Vanessa walked over to her co-teacher and placed a concerned hand on her shoulder.

"Vanessa…I don't know how to say this…" Mrs. Ritters burst into another round of tears. There was no way Vanessa was going to decode her blubbering. She walked over to her desk to turn on the television with the remote. Mrs. Ritters turned to walk down to Mr. Fitz's classroom to start the cycle again.

Vanessa sat on top of a student's desk.

"Dad," she gasped.

Kids started filing into the room.

"What are you watching, Miss Vanessa?"

Vanessa's trance finally broke from the news. She stood and looked behind her to see all of her students' worried faces.

"Hey look," a kid applauded, "It's Sam's mom…the news reporter."

"Oh, yeah!"

"So cool!"

The kids chimed in.

Just then, another plane crashed into the second tower of the World Trade Center.

"Ahhh."

"Is this for real?"

"Is this happening now?"

The children panicked; some were crying and others froze, just staring at the television. Vanessa immediately turned off the T.V. The kids crowded around Miss Vanessa, looking for answers and comfort.

The PA system crackled on, then the principal spoke, "Given the events of today thus far, all buses are reassembling to take the children back home. We have already notified the parents. Teachers, please assist your classrooms to the bus lanes as calmly as possible. I know you all have family to get to as well." He signed off with another crackle of the PA system.

Vanessa ran to the doorway, blocking the children in so that she could get a headcount before they ran out, then she led them into the hallway. The sea of students was flowing out of their homerooms and headed to the double doors at the end of the hallway. Older siblings searched for their younger brothers or sisters and hugged them.

Vanessa herded her students to those parents who were still out front talking with other parents after dropping their kids off or those who had heard of the tragic news and rushed to the school. She then proceeded to the buses to send off the rest of the children who had their parents waiting for them at home. Once everyone was accounted for, she raced to Brian's home…her childhood home.

She turned on the radio. "This just in, a fourth plane has crashed down onto a field near Stoney Creek Township confirming a total of four crashes: two into the Trade Centers, one into the Pentagon, and now the field."

"Shit." Vanessa pulled up to Brian's house. His car was already gone. She pulled out her cellphone and called the firehouse, but the phones weren't working.

She rushed to the Trade Centers. She figured she would do what she could to help contain the fire and hoped to find her dad while doing so.

The closer she got to the city, the worse the traffic got. The road had become a parking lot. Vanessa sat in her car. "How am I going to get there?" She hit the steering wheel with her fist. "I can't help if I can't get there," she yelled.

She looked in her rearview mirror. The sparrow had been following her all day. Vanessa opened the door, got out, then slammed it shut.

"What do you want from me?" she shouted at the bird. She threw her hands up, not caring about the other passengers who were watching her. "You have followed me around for all these years…for what? Nothing good has ever stayed around long enough for you to see me as happy as you claim you wish me to be! You said you gave me this so-called gift…," she paused as she picked up her necklace to show her mother, "because you just wanted to spend more time with me? Well, Mother, how is that working out for you? How much time have we actually spent together bonding as mother and daughter? My sadness and anger toward you have created a barrier between us that you caused in the first place. And all my lives have ended tragically and far too early to have spent much time with you anyway. I can't honestly say that I've ever lived a full life. Is that what you wanted? You have removed balance in the world for your own selfish reasons and there isn't one person who has benefited. Not. One. The best thing you could've done was to stay with Father in the first place, then none of this would have ever happened!"

Vanessa paused her ranting as she noticed people getting out of their cars, so she turned around. Cries and screams pierced the air as the North Tower collapsed onto the rubble of the already fallen South Tower. Smoke bellowed and soon covered their road in a dark blanket of gray.

She joined the chaos by continuing her rant to her mother.. "You have caused this." Vanessa held up her arms, showing the destruction and despair-stricken faces of people who had loved ones in those buildings. "It's your fault because you wanted to still be a part of my life even though you are the one who left in the first place. You gave me this…this fucking curse. You took the love, kindness, and forgiveness out of this world, so I may live and be part of your life. What you failed to see or learn is that we need balance. All of your actions have consequences, whether you are magical, human, good, or the fucking dark fairy queen."

Vanessa crumpled to her knees. The hard pavement didn't even bother her. Vanessa continued to sob, wishing she could absorb all the pain from the surrounding people.

"Not only have you brought hate and destruction to this world…my world…" She sniffed before her nose leaked like her eyes were. Her chest spasmed trying to catch her breath from all of her sobbing. "You brought pain and sadness to these innocent people. Right now, they are losing their parents, brothers and sisters, husbands and wives, friends…they are all gone. You sacrificed thousands of lives, for just one. Mine. And I hate you for taking that from them."

Vanessa's spirit shattered into millions of pieces, like glass crushed and ground down to a powder. In that moment, when the world around her had been ripped at its seams, she remembered all of her lost loved ones.

She remembered playing with Lucian in their forest fairyland after they had completed her studies. She missed her conversations with her knight in shining armor, her first genuine friend.

Even though Marcus had killed her in the end, her time with him wasn't all bad. Food fights and painting were not just a treat, but their daily lives—such freedom she had felt. The fact she could give Cristina the resources to start a new life brought joy to Vanessa's heart.

Mama Helen, though misunderstood by the village people, was kind natured, and lived solely to help others. Her dear friend Millie, innocent by definition, had looked up to Vanessa as more than a friend, but a sister and role model.

Miss Hughes had found enough love to guide children to new loving homes. And Shirley may not have had the best moral compass, but she was the friend Vanessa needed at that time in her many lives.

"I had love in my heart once," Vanessa whispered.

The sparrow, now at her knees, looked up at her daughter's face.

"My James," Vanessa touched her scarred heart. The bump of her unique burn jolted up her spine with piercing pins and needles. She could only imagine the suffering the victims of this current attack were going through.

"I can't do this anymore." She brushed the butterfly pendant with her fingers before clenching it into her fist. The bird jumped around and chatted with urgency as Vanessa pulled the necklace up over her head. Vanessa tossed it into the smog. The necklace dissolved, and its particles joined the sooty air.

The sparrow jumped into Vanessa's lap, settling into the crack of her pressed legs. After minutes of Vanessa's tears dropping onto the sparrow's feathers, Vanessa looked out into the midst of New York City as its people scrambled away from the danger, fear and heartbreak of its most painful day. People rushed past her desperately looking for loved ones, answers, and help. In the coming days, they would be looking for comfort…looking for hope.

Vanessa pried her heavy eyes open. Stark white walls surrounded her.

Beep…Beep…Beep…Beep

A monitor tracked her heartbeat, which Vanessa thought to be paced a bit slow.

She glared as she looked towards the window. The sun didn't shine its brightest. How could it? The air was still in a thick haze of smoke and dust.

"Vanessa," a voice sheepishly called.

Vanessa shifted her focus to the chair in the corner of her hospital room.

"Mother," Vanessa's voice cracked. Vanessa shifted to a sitting position, wondering if she should fear Selena's wrath for throwing away the "gift" she had given her.

"Please, save your strength. I'm not here to harm you, nor am I here to change your mind."

Selena was in her human form. Vanessa thought she was quite pretty though it was odd seeing her in jeans and a T-shirt.

"I never understood your perspective—never realized how selfish I had been. I am deeply sorry for assuming you'd have an icy heart like me. I knew from the moment you were born you were more like your father—which is why I left. How could I raise you to be like me when you were so clearly not. I had hoped that over time, you'd change. You were close in the 1920s." She chuckled lightly at the memory of her daughter enjoying the frivolities of that time. Selena reached for her daughter's hand and was relieved when Vanessa allowed it.

Vanessa looked at their hands and noticed how aged hers appeared, wrinkled and veiny, especially compared to her mother's. Gradually, she looked up at her mother. "Am I dying?"

Selena lifted Vanessa's hand to her lips and gave it a gentle peck.

"Lillian told me I would just die a natural death eventually. What's happening?"

"Unfortunately, Lillian is a child at heart and has always been jealous of my love for you. She told you what you wanted to hear. She's not mature enough to know this kind of magic to its fullest extent. Lillian didn't know what the outcome would be. She just knew she needed you out of her way to get my attention."

Selena laid Vanessa's hand back on the cold sheets and walked over to the window.

"I loved your father dearly, Vanessa. He made me want to have a family. I did not know this was going to be the outcome of our union. I guess I wasn't much of a mother to you or your sister."

Selena turned to look at her daughter. Vanessa's eyes sunk into her skeleton-like face. Her skin looked like aged leather, worn and wrinkled. She was ashy in color, and one could see her collar and cheek bones.

"You are indeed fading, my butterfly. It's just not a peaceful death like Lillian fooled you into believing. After taking this necklace off..." Selena dangled the pendant, watching it as it spun around, untangling its cord. "your lives have caught up with you. Your body systems are failing you one by one. You have another day…maybe."

Selena tossed the necklace right in front of Vanessa's resting fingertips.

"How did you–?"

Selena drummed her fingers in the air. "Magic."

Vanessa couldn't help but slowly move her head side to side, questioning her mother's angle with a new necklace.

"I love you, Vanessa, but I will no longer keep you locked in a cage of sorrow. I leave this choice up to you. You can stop your suffering and replace this necklace around your neck, or you can save this world and your humans from any unnecessary darkness. I won't stop you either way, and neither will Lillian; you can be sure of that. I hope you can find it in your heart to forgive me before you pass, whenever that may be, but I know I don't deserve that gift from you."

Selena blew a kiss from her stance at the window then rubbed her fingers together. The queen fairy shined brightly and left through the tiny crack in the window's framing.

Knock, Knock

The door opened and a set of eyes peaked in.

"Dad." Vanessa tried to move to get out of bed, but she couldn't find the will nor the energy.

"Stay in bed, baby girl." Brian rushed to her side.

"You're alive," Vanessa whimpered.

"I've been working since it happened, pulled an all-nighter. They couldn't find my location to inform me of your state; otherwise, I would have been here sooner. What happened to you?"

Vanessa could tell Brian had exhausted every muscle in his body. He coughed, trying to clear the smoke and debris from his lungs. His shoulders were heavy. The pressure to find every last body had him feeling defeated. He wanted to be here with his daughter, but he knew he needed to help the survivors try to find their missing loved ones.

"Dad, I'm sick. I've been sick for some time now. I just didn't want you to worry."

"You're my daughter. I have a right to worry."

"You are also a firefighter. You have a duty, dad. Those victims need you more than I do. I'm ready for whatever happens, and I've found my peace. You should help others find theirs."

"I knew you were special the moment I picked you up. This bird was watching me while I read the note that was attached to your blanket."

"Note?" Vanessa never remembered a note in her past lives.

"There was a note signed by whom I am assuming was your biological mother." He dug into the many pockets of his fire suit and finally pulled out his wallet. He uncrumpled the note he had kept all those years.

Brian laid the note on Vanessa's chest so she could read it at her leisure.

She really has changed.

Vanessa looked at her dad and smiled. She had a choice to make, and Brian had families to reunite.

"Thank you for this, Dad. Thank you for everything. I love you."

"I love you too, Vanessa."

"Now go do what you do best. Go help those families." Vanessa reassured him it was alright to leave.

"Okay, but I'll be back tonight or tomorrow morning to check on you." He kissed her forehead, then walked out the door.

"If I'm still here," she breathed.

Her hand shook as she inched her fingertips towards the pendant, which still sat next to her on the bed. Vanessa felt the bumps of the stones and ridges that framed the details of the butterfly. She then read the note from Selena that her father had left for her to read. After reading what her mother had to say, she turned to face the window, still resting her head on the pillow, and closed her eyes. She could feel all the pain…all the hate that had built up over centuries.

The following night, Brian kept his promise and visited his daughter. But when he entered the room, Vanessa was already gone. A pile of dust sat on the bed with a cord and a few purple and green stones that still glimmered in the sun's light.

Epilogue

September 2011

Brian stood at the edge, viewing the names of the firemen whom he had lost on 9/11. He looked up to gaze at the surrounding crowd, mourning their loved ones.

A butterfly flew up to him and landed on his finger that was touching the engraved placard.

"Hello, lovely. Aren't you lovely? Such a rare-looking sort–and yet…somehow familiar." As he admired the butterfly that seemed strangely attached to him, he noticed its wings were a burnt gold, almost rust-colored. The shape of the bottom wings was pointed and uneven. A black stripe intruded the golden sections, eventually separating the gold from a dusted glitter of emerald–a green that matched the rich moss in the depths of a fairytale forest.

The two watched families say hello, and then their goodbyes to the fallen.

Brian moved to leave, but studied his little friend as it stayed perched on his finger, gently fanning its wings and returning the look of intensity. Finally, he faintly smiled and as a tear trickled down his cheek, he said, "Such sorrow is soaked into the ground under this memorial. May you never experience such pain."

He lifted his hand, and the butterfly took off, gliding into the sunset.

"So you're finally letting her go?" Lillian smirked as she walked up to her fairy-mother, who was watching Vanessa fly away from a nearby tree.

"I did what I could." Selena hung her head. "I guess I wasn't the greatest mother to either of you."

"At least you know it now. What was it about Vanessa that made you push me aside, anyway?"

"There are powers beyond this world that you can't even begin to fathom, my child. To be honest, I knew I didn't have to worry about you. You took after me after all. In a witch's life… Well, she wouldn't be as protected."

Selena looked at Lillian, who was watching the sunset in the distance. Selena knew she was talking to a wall at this point. "I guess I don't have to worry about her anymore. She was too good, just like your father."

"You know what? Enough about witches. You and I have a long life together now. I have a lot of time to catch up with you…that is, if you can forgive me?"

Lillian's dark blue aura seemed to crack allowing for a more brilliant sapphire to shine through. Uncharacteristically, Lillian timidly asked, "I would have you to myself?"

Selena nodded and smiled. She went up to Lillian and hugged her. "Yes."

"Finally." Lillian regained her composure, ashamed of her temporary emotional weakness, and blamed her sister for it. After watching her for so many years, some of the kind witchy essence must have rubbed off. "Well, it's about time." She released her embrace from her mother and adjusted her clothing.

"On one condition." Selena, remembering Lillian's previous ways, quickly warned, "Do not eat your sister. I know your blue jay's taste for rare butterflies, but your sister is off limits. Deal?"

Lillian raised an eyebrow, making Selena's heart race, but then Lillian smiled. "Deal," she said as she giggled. Selena relaxed and shook her head.

The two fairies darted off and their glow sparkled as the brightest stars against the sky as it continued to change from soft pinks, into a fiery red and orange and eventually faded into the dark blue of a night sky as the sun took its rest.

About the Author

Callie Rae Sutton is a short story author who has been published in three previous *"Of Words"* anthologies published by Scout Media. Her first self publication was "The Collection of Thirteen" which is comprised of thirteen short stories of various genres.

Callie is a wife and a teacher to both her preschool students and her daughter.

Fantasy, mythology, and crime tend to be her choices of poisons, however, she also dabbles in adventure and love stories with a twist.

Be sure to visit her at:
www.blushingcrow13.com

9 7 9 8 9 8 8 5 5 3 9 2 2